Hamster Stories

or

'A tenuous grip on reality'

Ruler's Wit

Ex Libris

Cathie Hasler

RW

Ruler's Wit

For hamsters everywhere, and their chosen humans.

Why hamster tales? – Why not?

At a team meeting we were discussing some unfortunate incidents that had happened, which were humorous, and one involved a hamster and a face-plant across the floor. And that's where the idea began.

Hamsters are rodents belonging to the subfamily Cricetinae, which contains nineteen species classified in seven genera. The best-known species of hamster is the golden or Syrian hamster, which is the type most commonly kept as a pet. Who knew? Well, some of our authors did.

The stories in the anthology did not have to be about a hamster, or hamsters, there just needed to be a tenuous link to the little rodents. The stories are all owned by their authors who keep the copyright. All views are the author's own. There seems to be a presumption that hamsters are escape artists, but let's just say, they don't all get away.

There is a prize, worth £50, for the winning author, but the stories are not being judged by the Ruler's Wit team, they are being judged by you, the reader. The winning author will be able to choose from: a book cover design; proofreading or copy-editing of 2,000 words; development edit of 2,000 words; mentoring or writing of a blog post.

When you have read and enjoyed the anthology, please

vote for your favourite story by 31 January 2025 and the one with the most votes will be the prize winner. You can vote on our website, by direct message through our Facebook page, or you can email.

We hope you will enjoy reading tales of hamsters and tales with just a tenuous link.

The Rulers Wit team
www.rulerswit.co.uk
hello@rulerswit.co.uk

Contents

An Uncommon Obsession

Jenni Dobson

It was probably due to his grandmother that Johnny Pritchett had such an interest in magic and witches, but even so he wasn't prepared to meet a witch right there on the first day of a new school year.

Of course it wasn't immediately apparent to anyone else that his new teacher was a witch, but Johnny was convinced of it at once. For a start, he thought no ordinary person could be quite so beautiful. It must be an illusion to deceive people. Underneath was probably an ugly old woman – but to all appearances ....

He had heard Gran talk of 'skin like ivory' and thought that now he knew what she meant.

Then there was her hair. To call it red was not enough; it made him think of the sun shining on Gran's copper ornaments, of autumn leaves tossed in the breeze, but most of all, of the leaping flames in Gran's fireplace. Then there were her eyes – a vivid breath-taking green, cat-like and compelling – even now burning into him and knowing that he knew.

The clincher came when one of his classmates asked which of them would be taking the hamster home to look after for the weekend. She had explained, kindly it's true, that Loki wasn't a class pet in the usual way. He was hers and she would always take him home with her at weekends. He's her familiar, that's why, thought Johnny.

He was sure that he was right about her. You had only to see the magical way the children clustered around her – charmed by her looks and exotic flowing clothes, fascinated by her voice and stories, spellbound absolutely. Only Johnny stayed aloof, quietly doing his lessons, finding other ways to amuse himself at break, giving her no chance to get even with him – for knowing.

'Gran,' he said one day, 'how would you tell if someone was a witch?' He could ask Gran anything and she never turned a hair.

'Well,' she replied, 'I don't think that'd be easy, do you? Because they could use all that magic and witchcraft to hide behind, couldn't they? I did read once upon a time they used to try people they thought were witches by fire and by water. I don't remember exactly – but they had a thing called a ducking stool and the witch was tied to it and ducked under the water. If you drowned you were innocent, but if you could stay under water so long and come out still alive, then you must be a witch – and so they burned you!'

Johnny's face was creased in a frown.

'Seems to me you couldn't win either way, Gran,' he said eventually. 'Seems that way to me too, Johnny,' came the answer.

One playtime he was collecting seeds when unexpectedly he saw her, pacing up and down on the path outside the staffroom French windows. The air was filled with a strange smell.

She spotted him too at the same moment and stopped, but instead of telling him to return to the playground, she looked rather 'caught in the act' – as Gran would say. Then he saw the reason for the strange smell. She was smoking.

She made a face at him, saying, 'So it had to be you who discovers my guilty secret.'

Somehow, he felt that recognised the different knowledge they had of each other – that he knew she was a witch and that she knew that he knew.

He looked at the cigarette between her fingers. She looked down at it too. It was not the kind of cigarette he had seen before. It was very thin and tatty – it looked about to fall to bits.

'Yes, I know I ought to give it up,' she began, 'but they are herbal ones. Even so, the rest of them,' with a jerk of her head towards the staffroom, 'won't let me smoke in there.

Perhaps I should find a herbal remedy to help me to give them up. I'm quite into herbs and things, you know.'

He did know. There had been an episode when she had arrived at school in a strange green dress she had dyed herself and she had brought bags full of nettles for the children to cook up a dye bath. Mr Henty, the headmaster, had demanded

3

to know what was the smell and what did it have to do with the National Curriculum? She had said, 'Weighing and measuring, and a bit of chemistry.' And Mr Henty had nothing left to say.

Somehow, brewing up a pot of nettles then adding different things to change the colour seemed rather tame for a witch, but he supposed she had to be careful that people didn't catch on. Maybe she wanted to see if there might be any budding witches in his class. Certainly they had the best display when it came to decorating the classroom for Hallowe'en. They bobbed for apples in a bowl – being careful not to drown because Mr Henty wouldn't like that – she had warned the children, and while they did it, she entertained them with all kinds of tales and superstitions. Johnny wondered what she would do when Christmas came.

It turned out to be better than Santas made from cardboard tubes and felt. They made fat gingerbread men to hang on the tree, and while they decorated them, she read to them the story of the Gingerbread Man who came to life. For their part in the school concert, she wrote a scene for the class to tell about the Christmas tree, how it was a pagan symbol taken over by the Christians and how Queen Victoria's husband had brought the tradition over from Germany. They thought it was much more fun than yet another load of shepherds dressed in bath towels tied up with clothes lines, and they played their parts with gusto.

Johnny reflected that it had certainly been an interesting and unusual term and over the Christmas holiday he found himself missing his new teacher. Of course, it wasn't that he liked her, but he missed not having her to watch. For he had decided he would have to watch her closely in the New Year if he was really to prove that she was a witch.

From keeping out of her way he had gradually become her shadow, watching, waiting, certain that one day the time would come when beyond all doubt everyone would know.

The days lengthened and they moved into the season for outings. Johnny's class went on a trip to a fairy tale castle, complete with a moat full of water and towers at the corners. His teacher had changed her dark clothes of winter for an outfit of warm, golden orangey colours, as if in celebration of the spring.

Leaving the main group below, Johnny tramped up a tower stairway behind her, thinking it was exactly how a good castle ought to be, itching to reach the top and look out, imagining himself to be the lord and master of it all.

They reached the top breathlessly and gazed over the parapet.

'Phew, after that I need a ciggie,' she said. 'You won't tell on me, will you, Johnny?'

He drew back, shaking his head, moving towards the stairs. If she was going to light up one of those smelly things, he would clear off and leave her to pollute the clean, sweet breeze alone. He heard her behind him, clicking her lighter and exclaiming in annoyance.

'This wind! Come on, you brute, light!'

He turned to see her fiddling with the lighter, clicking it again and again. 'Light! Light!' she snarled through clenched teeth.

The flame suddenly leapt up, licking at her vibrant red curls. She gasped, recoiling from the lighter, the cigarette falling from her lips. She tried to turn her hair away from the wind but it tossed her glowing curls in all directions. He watched horrified as she beat at them wildly, twisting and turning this way and that – then suddenly she was over the edge.

He flung himself at the stonework, and looking down, saw her falling, her brilliant curls, her flowing amber dress, whirling like some great Catherine wheel. She seemed to take forever to fall.

Finally, there came a splash as she reached the moat. That sound released a deafening racket: the rushing of the wind about his head, roaring blood in his ears and from everywhere screams, screams, screams.

Two men jumped into the water. Someone threw a lifebelt from the bridge over the moat. The shocked and stunned school party were taken away to a quieter place until they were able to leave for home.

As they walked back to their coach, Johnny overheard a snatch of conversation. 'Oh no, it wasn't the fall nor the flames that did it, it seems she drowned.'

'Who will look after her hamster now?'

Hamster Dreaming:
A Tenuous Grip on Reality

Emily Gentry

Drew took a few deep breaths as he nervously stared at the blank page.

'Drew, it's okay, just take your time,' Harry said. Harry was such a great comfort to Drew, especially when things got too much for him. It's funny because Harry wasn't even Drew's friend, he was his younger brother's friend, but he was kind to everyone who met him, and just had a knack of saying the right thing just when it was needed.

Drew put pencil to paper and began. First, he drew a large round body, like a potato, a furry potato. No sounds but the scratching of pencil crayon on paper in Drew's bedroom, as they both concentrated on the image he was creating. Grabbing another colour, from the selection strewn across his bed, the furry potato now had red eyes, long sharp fangs, razor- sharp claws and something of a sinister smile.

'A hamster?' Harry sounded almost insulted at this realisation. 'Yes but believe me, this thing is terrifying.' Drew stressed.

'Sure, OK,' and Harry composed himself, remembering that he was trying to be supportive. 'What is so scary about this hamster?' he calmly probed.

'Every time I have the same nightmare. It's always this thing chasing me.' Drew jabbed at the drawing. 'It starts with the sound of his breathing, fast and snuffly. Then I'm beginning to panic because I know he's coming, so I start running but he's so quick. And I'm running and running but not getting any further away from him.'

'How big is this hamster?' Harry wondered, still a little sceptical about a hamster's ability to strike fear into the heart of a fully grown adult. To Harry, Drew seemed so grown up, but at twenty-five, Drew still felt adolescent, lost and uncertain of himself.

'He's bigger than me! But then, this is where it gets really bad, I look back and see his face is no longer a hamster face with whiskers and red eyes, it's now my face on this giant hamster body, and I'm petrified, and start screaming and screaming. Then I wake up.

Sweating and completely freaked out.'

There, he said it. It might sound pathetic, it did to Drew, but he felt a little relief at vocalising this problem that had been plaguing him for months, and he sat back to catch his breath. His room wasn't big, and the crammed-full bookshelves overhanging his bed made it feel even smaller.

'OK, that does sound scary,' Harry agreed, and he reached out to his open packet of crisps and ate in quiet contemplation.

Drew and his brother didn't really know much about Harry's background, or his parents, he couldn't really talk about it but they knew he was happy hanging out with them at their little flat, and they always had plenty of food for him to snack on and he was a good listener so they didn't pry.

'Same dream every time you say?' Harry has an idea. Drew nodded. 'OK, why don't you practise changing the ending? You know, see if you can subconsciously plant into the nightmare a better ending, so you could maybe turn around and Kung-Fu evil hamster into oblivion.'

'No, I'm no good at martial arts.' Drew replied matter-of-factly.

'Drew, it doesn't have to be real, it's a dream!' Harry was a little exasperated at having to explain this. 'You could turn into a giant raspberry and squish him, or fly him into the sun, or play pat-a-cake with him, anything at all.'

'I don't think my brain would let me do that, it needs at least a tenuous grip on reality.' 'OK, what are you good at, what do you enjoy doing?'

There was only one thing Drew really enjoyed in life, but it was bittersweet. He loved writing, or in truth he loved the idea of writing. Day-to-day life wasn't easy for Drew, his work was unfulfilling and socially he was awkward. He found it hard to keep up with friendships, people were exhausting and confusing, but equally he needed people. He was fascinated by them and often wished he could write about their lives in an eloquent way, expand his ideas and just communicate spellbindingly, skilfully. But the sad reality was that he didn't know a noun from an adjective, and never made it past half a first chapter before losing confidence and confining his concepts to forgotten files, titled 'Story Idea'.

Normally, Drew would be too embarrassed to talk about this, even to his brother, but it was different with Harry, who didn't interrupt and just let him talk and talk until his worries began to make sense.

'I love to write stories,' Drew answered. 'But I've never got anywhere with it, it's a bit of a fear of mine to actually pursue it in anyway.' There was a deep panic that would rise up in Drew every time he thought about it. So many obstacles in his way, it made him feel dizzy at the prospect of navigating through. First, the impossible task of catching those fleeting ideas swirling around his mind; how could he turn them into anything coherent on paper? The frustration was followed by the agoraphobia of breaching the real world, who would his audience be, who would he write for, what format did they want? And finally, the avoidance tactic to ease the discomfort, and it all went away until the niggle to write arose again and again.

Harry's eyes lit up. 'Well that's it! Drew, when evil hamster starts coming for you, pull out a pen and start rewriting the ending, take back that control.' Harry was excited but Drew was yet to be convinced.

'Maybe.' He shrugged and went back to adding detail to his drawing. They sat in silence for a moment, but for the scratching of pencil and crunching of crisps.

'Drew?' Harry had another idea. 'What if this is your nightmare?'

At Harry's words, that familiar tingle of dread spread through Drew from his head to his toes. Slowly, he put down the pencil and knowingly, dared to look across at Harry. Oh no, Harry was swiftly expanding into the giant furry potato of his drawing, now looming over him with red eyes and sharp claws. Drew jumped up from his bed and ran to the door but knew the hamster monster was hot on his heals and gaining pace. Not again, he thought as he ran through the streets of his neighbourhood.

'Drew, come back, it's OK,' shouted giant-hamster, Harry.

'Wait! What?' This wasn't how it played out every other time. And he slowed to a walk, looking back.

'I know what your nightmare means, let me be your guide.' Giant-hamster guru, Harry, was so reassuring that Drew stopped completely and couldn't help but listen, his hands on his hips, trying to catch his breath as his heart still pounded fast.

'Stop running, Drew.'

'I have, Harry.'

'No, I mean stop running from yourself.' Giant-hamster guru, Harry had Drew's face, just like in the usual nightmare, only this time he wasn't fierce and his eyes were green, just like his own. 'Don't be afraid to try. Make mistakes, fail and learn from them. Start writing,

Drew, it's OK, you might completely suck at it, but it's better to try and fail than have unfulfilled regret. That's living, don't be afraid to live.'

Drew woke up with a jolt, his eyes wide open and alert, sweat itching down his back, and out of breath.

'Hamsters,' he muttered to himself as he started laughing quietly. It must have been so early in the morning it was still dark outside. He scrabbled around his bookcase for a new notebook, found one with only a few pages used for shopping lists, which he tore out and scrawled across the new first page, Story Idea. For a few seconds, he looked at his two short words and quickly scribbled out the word Idea. This time it wasn't going to be just an idea, something that stayed locked in his mind, no, this time his story would come to fruition.

Good or bad, something was going to be created. He got up to get a glass of water, tiptoed past his brother's room and stopped to smile at Harry through the partially open door.

'Thank you, Harry,' he whispered, as Harry sat in his wheel, amongst his sawdust bed and washed his face with his hands. For a moment, Harry looked up from licking his hands, his little pink eyes met with Drew's for a brief second, before setting off at a run as the wheel squeaked to each rotation. It didn't wake Drew's brother, he was used to it.

This night, for the first time, Drew felt an excitement within him that wasn't accompanied by crippling anxiety. He had a tingle of hope that if he started this ball rolling and failed, that it didn't matter too much, because for the first time he felt the joy of just writing for writing's sake. And although there were many more nightmares to come that haunted Drew's sleep, this particular nightmare never visited him again.

Rupert

Emma Villiers

It's exactly a thousand days since I died. That's two years and two-hundred-and-seventy days; not that I'm counting, not really. I only know this because the Earth is one gigantic clock. If I concentrate hard enough, I can literally hear the planet tick; humans have this ridiculous obsession with time. I should know, I used to be one.

I press my energy against the hamster cage and feel a warm glow as a familiar pink nose pokes out of the little brown house and sniffs at the air. Of course he can't smell me, but he knows I'm here. Rupert was just a baby when I took my last breath, a tiny ball of butterscotch fur, with inquisitive pink eyes. I remember him standing on his hind legs with his head cocked to one side, watching curiously as I was felled in one fatal swoop. My lifeless body swallowed by the shaggy white rug, my blood turning the faux fur an angry, sticky red. Now the space beneath his cage is bare, the rug rotting in some forensic closet somewhere,

unwanted. Rupert's eyes are darker and he moves with less speed now. In what's been the blink of an eye for me, he's gotten old.

There's a rumble behind me and I turn to see the now lanky frame of my brother slope in, collapsing on the two-seater with a pizza spilling over a small plate. He flicks on the TV without even a glance my way. Believe me, I've gone to town on all the clichés: changing channels, messing with the temperature, shorting the lights. Frankly, I'm exhausted. Not to mention that all this is completely frowned upon. I flick my gaze upwards, seriously, what are they going to do, kill me? I hover my hand over the TV remote and focus, it flicks onto Naked Attraction, and I'm satisfied to see Steven recoil at the sight of six flaccid willies.

Swearing, he fumbles with the control and flicks it back to Top Gear, but I notice he's gone a little pale and the remote trembles in his sweaty grip. OK, pranking Steven is not why I'm here, but I need him alert, receptive.

The atmosphere shifts again, and my stepfather's imposing frame appears, before dropping next to Steven and gently draping an arm across the top of the sofa, just above his thin shoulders. Outside the sun is slowly sloping back to bed, yawning a warm honey glow across the room. Steven stirs and I realise he's been asleep. So much for alert.

'You know I'm seeing Asa tomorrow. Sure you don't want to come?' My stepfather's voice is gentle, he picks at some dried blue paint on his work trousers and waits with a patience curated by time, but it's laden with something –

grief? No, not that.

Steven doesn't reply, he just stares at the TV without seeing it, the pizza cold on his lap.

'What you doing up, mate?'

The paint forgotten, my stepfather hoiks up his trousers and leans towards Rupert's cage, but the hamster blanks him, instead scurrying over to where I am. Rising up on his hind legs, front paws hooked, he cocks his head and looks at me with those deep red eyes.

'I'm sure he misses our Katie.'

The acknowledgement is an instant charge to my energy. Rupert flinches, dropping onto all fours.

'Silly thing.' My stepfather chuckles and settles back in his seat.

Steven doesn't move, but I see the energy around him harden, the thickening of a shell. He's disintegrating before me, before our stepfather. I can see his paths unfolding, all his possible futures, a spider web of them and in every one, he's the fly.

'You know, mate,' my stepfather lets out a breath and rubs his hands up and down his ample thighs, 'you were like this when your mother left. That clever brain of yours whirling nine to the dozen, trying to process a situation it just didn't have a contingency for.'

Steven doesn't speak, but his eyes are blinking rapidly and the fingers of his left hand twitch – all the while the shell is getting denser.

'You, Katie, Asa, barely out of nappies the three of you.

Blimey it was tough.' With the cuff of his shirt he wipes at red-rimmed eyes. 'But we got through it, mate, because we are a team.'

Tentatively, his hand reaches out but stops just short of touching Steven. His voice is gentle, coaxing.

'Asa made a mistake, didn't he, mate?'

Steven's fingers move so fast they are almost vibrating, he crushes them into his palm. 'Mate?'

Then I see it. The rug is back. I'm there, falling. My right hand cradling the left jugular. A waterfall of crimson rushing through my fingers. Without a flicker of emotion, I watch as my former body hits the floor with an undignified thump. My mouth flickers open and shut, but I only managed a sticky gurgling sound, before my eyes fix and my pupils dilate. There's something else, a noise. Sound fills the room around us, looping and swirling, over and over, and I realise that's all he is hearing – the last sound I make. Steven squeezes his eyes shut against the memory, covers his ears, rocking back and forth. The image flickers like an old cine tape, but there's a crack in the shell.

Come on Steven.

My stepfather has shifted position, I didn't see him move, but he's now crouched in front of my brother. This is it.

'You know it's a thousand days since our Katie died, mate, exactly a thousand days today?'

He lets the significance land.

Steven's eyes finally flicker up, only for the briefest of seconds, but it's enough.

'I kept seeing the number everywhere today. Order forms,

measurements, invoices ... the lads on site told me to see a shrink ...'

He lets the words hang.

'It took me a while, Steven, I know I'm not the sharpest tool,' he lets out an embarrassed cough, 'but, well, mate, I had to ask myself why would it matter like? A thousand days, two thousand, who cares really, she's gone.'

He takes a breath, glances over his shoulder, watches as Rupert scales the bars to the top hatch, where I'd always let him out.

'Then that proverbial penny dropped – the thousand days, they don't mean shit, Steven, nor do a thousand hours or minutes, but it's the seconds, mate, it's the bloody thousand seconds.'

My energy roars, filling the room and shorting the TV. There's a gentle thump as Rupert drops straight onto his back into the sawdust. My stepfather shivers and Steven begins to cry.

'Asa made a mistake, didn't he, boy?' Steven's mouthing something, we both see it.

'I'm sorry'.

Undeterred, Rupert's back, drilling down on the latch.

'You were her big brother by a thousand seconds. You used to wind her up something rotten with that when you were kids, "You'll always be a thousand seconds behind me, loser."' Our stepfather laughs at the memory.

The layers are peeling away.

The rug's back. But there's three of us now. Steven and I screaming at each other, our big brother on the sidelines, always the peacemaker.

There's icing sugar on my top and a knife in Steven's hand. He's furious. I'd iced some childish slur on the top of Asa's birthday cake. Ruined it, he'd screamed in my face. Then he spins and swipes a tumbler of water from the coffee table, he throws the water at me, but it catches my chin, the cheap glass shatters against my jaw, a piece slices into my neck, a knife through a peach. My hand tries to stem the leak, but it's fruitless.

'Asa didn't – I …' and then he's in my stepfather's arms, sobbing. 'I know, mate, I know.'

I watch as Asa stands up from my body, and then gently takes what's left of the tumbler from Steven's fingers.

'When the police come, let me do the talking.' Then the scene is gone.

Saving Private Sparkle
Donna Shepherd

'Why do they put it in a cage? And in the kitchen – the noise it made last night; I barely slept a wink,' Barney grumbled.

'Maybe if you got out more and ate less you wouldn't be so tired. I was out most of the day and the sun was hiding so I ended up exploring a bit further,' Bear replied as he gazed into the cage. 'Anyway, it's not a cage. It's a pink palace and it seems the little thing has no trouble sleeping in the daytime.'

'Yeah, I noticed that. Feel like waking it up? Maybe then it would sleep all night,' Barney reasoned, before sniffing loudly. 'It smells a bit and it only arrived yesterday.'

'No, that'd be mean. Like you said, it only arrived yesterday, so best let it sleep.'

'You said you explored a bit further,' Barney prompted as he got comfy on his cushion, 'Where did you get to?'

'I walked up the hill a bit, jumped the fence and looked at the gardens in those new houses. Then I jumped onto a wall the other side and dropped into the first one.'

'Did you see anyone we know?'

'Yeah, as it happens. As I returned, that funny looking pair were peering over the fence near the kitchen window ...'

'What? Looking in here?' Barney gasped.

'Yes, they must have been standing on the small shed in Ted's old garden––'

'Oh, it's a shame he's gone,' Barney interrupted, concern etched on his face. 'His bark would have soon scared them off.'

'Don't worry.' Bear reasoned. 'I doubt you'll meet them, and if they do happen to be around when you venture into the garden, you can always dart back in,'

'What could they possibly want to look in here––'

'Oi,' a deep voice interrupted. 'Will you two keep it down?' They both froze and stared around the otherwise empty room.

'Right, I know you heard that but, what the ...' Barney's words dangled in the air and both watched, wide-eyed as a bundle of white fluff emerged from the small pink hut nestled in the corner of the pink palace.

Bear stepped forward and sniffed it through the cage bars.

'Stop sniffing so hard,' said the voice as the white bundle started to shake and a small furry brown face appeared. 'It makes the sawdust fly about.'

'Wow, it speaks!' Barney exclaimed, standing up and scratching his ear with his back leg.

'Of course I do. You think you got the monopoly on communication?' Barney jumped onto the table and glanced at Bear, who shrugged.

'Never really thought about it,' said Barney. All three gazed expectantly at each other.

'Well, I speak and you two standing over the cage is a tad irritating, and let's be honest here, intimidating.'

'Gosh,' said Barney, stepping back a few paces and sitting down. 'I guess it must be.

Bear, move back a bit.'

'Yes, that is better. Thanks.'

'I'm Barney and this is Bear, and while we should be house cats, which I have to say would suit me just fine, Katy does like to let us out. It's all his fault as he is a real sun worshipper and likes to lie flat out on his back in the sun. In truth, he looks like he's been dropped from a helicopter. I've heard Katy call him Bear Loaf.' Barney chuckled. 'Anyway, that's fine when you have fair fur but because I'm grey I get way too hot and––'

'Good lord, Barney! Take a breath,' said Bear with a deep sigh. 'Understand now why I head outside?' He winked at the newcomer. 'There really is no need to bore the chap with all that on the first meeting. At least give him time to realise you rarely draw breath and to figure out an escape route before you start.'

'Charming,' Barney huffed as he tucked his paws under his chest and poked his tongue out at Bear. 'I'm only being friendly.'

'Nice to meet you both. I'm Hank, although you may hear them call me Sparkles.'

Hank coughed, before climbing onto the top of the bright pink felt bed. 'Bit of a mix-up at the rescue. You'd think the blumin' humans could tell the difference.'

'Ah, I was struggling to align the deep voice with the pink palace cage and general air of homely femininity.' Bear laughed at the expression on Hank's face. 'Fear not, mate. Us rescue men must stick together. As you can see,' Bear continued, 'we are cats. To be specific, we are British Shorthairs and met at the rescue centre. Thankfully, Katy, that's the lady who lives with us, adopted us and opted for blue beds in honour of our masculinity.'

'Funny.' Hank grimaced as he plucked a seed from his hanging treat tree and popped it into his mouth. 'Careful there, old chap,' he said, before chewing the seed loudly, 'almost ruptured a rib – is he always this amusing?' He pointed at Barney who was still sulking, his head resting on his in-turned paws.

'Yup, always. Well, he thinks he is.' Barney lifted his head, 'but I tend to just let it wash over me. We have been together a while.'

'As I was saying,' Bear continued with a pointed gaze at Barney, 'we are cats and our breed tend to stay indoors, although I am forever grateful that Katy recognised my boredom and introduced me to the outside. So much to see, and when the sun is out ...'

'I just don't get the attraction. Fresh water, food on demand ...' Barney gave a contented sigh. 'You just gotta look hungry––'

'Although,' Bear interrupted with a snort, 'how she falls for that with the bloody size of you.'

'And snuggly, soft and deep beds.' Barney ignored his friend. 'Why face the outside when it's so nice in here? There are even toys should the desire to play arise.'

'Which, as you can see, he rarely does,' said Bear with a grin at Hank, who grinned back.

'Oh, bugger off,' said Barney good naturedly. 'Come on then, Hank. Your turn.'

Hank finished chewing and cleared his throat. 'I'm a Syrian hamster and my genealogy can be traced back to southern Turkey. My great, great, great, great – keep going with the great for a long time,' he said and laughed. 'Grandparents came over years ago. You know, the usual, searching for something different and ended up being directly responsible for a large proportion of us here in the UK now.'

'Wow,' said Barney, 'that's amazing. I've no idea what my background is. Do you, Bear?'

'Nope, can't remember much before waking up at the shelter and having that lump dumped on me 'cause he was scared.'

'It was terrifying,' Barney appealed to Hank, who smiled reassuringly back at him. 'Getting left there was the worst thing that ever happened to me. I was so glad to see a familiar face ...'

'I seem to recall snarling at you.'

'Yes, but you soon came round to my charm and eventually stopped nudging me away.' Bear laughed. 'Only to keep warm. Those places are made of wood and retain no heat.' All three chuckled.

'Anyway,' said Hank, 'I, along with a load of young uns, got dumped by the canal in a plastic-type crate, and I only realised we'd been floating when someone screamed and we were scooped out.'

'Good grief!' exclaimed Barney, wide-eyed, 'I thought being left at the shelter was traumatic enough, while you survived an attempted murder.'

'Yes, it was rather awful and we all spent the night in some boxes with bedding and lots of food before being taken to the rescue. I was picked up by the lovely lady who worked there, brought me here and placed me in this lovely light kitchen.'

'And you are very welcome, and very safe,' said Bear, 'no raw meat eaters here.' He chuckled. 'It's just a shame you have to live in that abomination,' he added with a grin.

'Did I wake you last night?' Hank asked, ignoring the taunt. Both cats shook their heads a little too quickly. 'Only if I don't get on the wheel and run, I tend to gain weight pretty quickly.'

'Wonder if we can get you a slightly larger wheel, Barney?' Bear quipped.

'Stop going on about my weight. The vet told Katy I have bigger bones than you.'

'Belly, Barney,' Bear guffawed, 'the vet said you have a bigger belly than me.'

'I'm going to have to get up earlier – you two are funny. I've never come across amusing cats before. At the rescue, there was a mean old cat that prowled around unsupervised. God, the looks she used to throw at me.' Hank shuddered. 'You could just tell I'd have made a tasty mouthful for her.'

'Yuk.' Barney retched. 'Live food. Can there be anything worse than live food? I cannot imagine having to chase, contain and kill some poor creature. Nope.' Barney stretched out on the table and rolled onto his back. 'I am all for those wonderfully tasty, pate-type meals that Katy serves.'

'I must agree.' Bear stopped as a loud bang sounded from the patio doors. 'What the bloody hell was that?'

'No idea but can you go and check it out, please?' Barney whimpered.

'Ah yes, I forgot – add loud bangs to the list with sort out spiders, anything that flies, and bugs,' said Bear, raising an eyebrow at Hank before jumping onto the kitchen floor.

Hank ran across the floor of his palace and into the tube on the end. Barney watched in amazement as the small furry body pushed up along the length of the tube before popping out into a small clear room at the top of the tower situated above the main cage.

'Wow, that's impressive. I wondered what that tube was for. Can you see now?'

'Yup, great view from up here, although good job I'm not scared of heights,' said Hank as he peered down on Bear, who was crouched to the left of the patio door.

'What can you see?' Barney called.

'Nothing yet, but there is definitely something out there. The bushes on the right keep shaking and I think ... oh yes, it's that funny looking pair I was going to tell you about earlier. I've only seen them a couple of times and spoken once but they are odd, although she's got a strikingly pretty face. Hang on, they're moving round the side of the house.'

'Don't let them in, for God's sake!'

'Erm, Barney, we don't have a cat flap and Katy is out. Relax, they can't get in.'

Bear watched until he was sure the two intruders had left the garden before walking to the chair perfectly placed in the sunshine. 'Now, gentlemen,' he said, as he leapt onto the chair and then slowly circled until he found the best spot, 'that is enough excitement for one afternoon, and if you are getting up later for some laps in that wheel, then you ought to get some rest too, Hank,'

'That, my new friend, sounds like an excellent idea,' said Hank as he jumped into the tube and slid back down to his bedroom floor. Gathering his bedding together, he pushed it back into the small hut, before disappearing inside it.

'Well, okay, if you are sure that they can't get in,' said Barney, a slight tremor in his voice as he looked across at Bear, who had started snoring softly.

'Oh, right, well,' Barney muttered to himself, 'erm, probably best that I rest too.' Barney yawned and made his way to his favourite spot on the sofa, before settling down, his eyes crossing in contentment and completely oblivious of the two feline faces peering around the door into the room.

A door banged loudly, sending reverberations through the house.

'What, whooo,' Barney yelled, involuntarily leaping into the air and landing on the floor with a soft thud, his back arched and body ready for flight. 'Hey, what's going on?'

Bear had looked up at the noise and grinned at Barney.

'Who'd have known that a body of your size could have retained any of its natural athleticism. That leap was pretty impressive.'

'What was that noise?' Barney asked, trying to get his

muscles to unwind so that he could sit.

'Relax.' Bear nestled his paws under his chest, sank his head onto them and closed his eyes. 'It must have been the wind. Maybe there's an open window upstairs.'

Abandoning the attempt to sit, Barney walked, straight-legged over to Bear and placed his front paws on the chair upon which his friend was already breathing gently.

'Erm, Bear ...' Barney leant forwards and whispered in the other cat's ear. 'Katy always closes the windows. Remember, she makes a point of checking they are all closed, or at least on those catch-things, if there's an open window then there could be someone ...'

An unfamiliar creak sounded above their heads and both cats stared deeply into the other's eyes.

Barney was not prepared for the swiftness of Bear's reaction and was subsequently pushed backwards into a furry ball as Bear moved from supine to hyper-alert in one fluid movement.

Bear signalled for Barney to go to the lounge door before he set off at a low crouch for the doorway into the hall.

Barney stayed close to the wall as he skirted back through the kitchen and looked up at the pink palace cage, noting two black eyes staring back at him.

'Bear's gone to check what that bang was,' Barney whispered as he jumped onto the table. 'I'm sure it's okay but just stay here. I'll be back in a mo.'

'I'd offer to help,' Hank spread his paws, 'but there's very little someone of my size can feasibly hope to achieve in the case of an offensive. Good luck,' Hank murmured, as Barney leapt from the table and headed for the lounge door.

The house had a kind of wrap-around feel with the kitchen and lounge being accessible from the hallway. The door of the lounge was slightly ajar and Barney eased his body through the gap, before disappearing behind the sofa and appearing again at the opposite end of the room. As he peered around the side of the door, he caught sight of Bear's tail as it rounded the top of the stairs. Taking a deep breath, Barney started to climb the stairs, one at a time, his ears straining for the slightest unfamiliar sound.

At the top, Barney glanced into the bathroom before turning right. Bear's concerned face appeared from under the bed in the front bedroom.

'I've checked both front rooms and neither window was open but the door to Katy's office was closed,' said Bear, 'so I couldn't check that window.'

'I wonder if that's the window that is open,' mused Barney. 'Maybe she opened it this morning before she––'

A crash exploded from the kitchen.

'What the f––' Bear yelled, sprinting for the stairs with Barney in close pursuit.

Erupting through the kitchen door, both cats stopped abruptly at the sight of the pink palace on its side, with the tunnel separated from the roof and the door swinging open, back and forth.

'Ooooof,' said Barney as he thumped into Bear's rump.

'Good of you to join us,' said the pretty tabby cat sitting in front of the patio door, licking her left paw.

'Get out of our home,' Barney shouted, his fur on end and

tail pointed out like a spikey Christmas tree. He glanced at Bear, who, to all outward appearance, looked calm and relaxed. 'Can you see Hank?' Barney mouthed the words behind his paw at Bear who twitched his nose and gave a gentle shake of his head.

'Seriously,' growled Bear, settling himself on his haunches, 'You dare to break in...'

'There was no break-in, was there, Bart?' the tabby cat interrupted.

Bear and Barney looked around the room.

A high-pitched laugh echoed throughout the room as a second cat, this time completely black but with a very damaged left ear, emerged from the folds of the curtain.

'Well, hello chaps. Bart is indeed my name, and no, we did not break in. We merely availed ourselves of the open window.'

'And you felt that was a good-enough signal to just step inside, did you?' said Bear.

'Looked like an invite to me and after all, we, that's my good friend, Savannah and I, wanted to get better acquainted with the rodent.'

'Yes, I did notice the carnage you've caused,' said Bear, indicating Hank's damaged home. 'I take it he managed to avoid your clutches?'

'For now,' said Bart, his eyes scanning the room. 'Anyway, you never mentioned you had a house guest when we saw you earlier.'

Bear ignored this, his own eyes glancing furtively left and right, resting on Barney who was still spiked up and hyper-alert.

'Try to relax,' Bear murmured, 'Hanks's safe. Do not look at it but he's under the fridge.'

'What you two whispering about?' said Bart, taking a couple of steps forward. 'You can't tell me you want to protect the rat? I know it's small but we could play with it a while––'

'Get out of our home!' Barney yelled, determined to avoid looking right at the fridge.

From the corner of his left eye, he saw Hank give him the thumbs up before disappearing back under the fridge.

'Oh, relax, furball,' said Savannah, 'I ain't here for you. I want that tasty-looking rodent. 'We seen it earlier through the window, so help us find it and we'll be off.'

'Furball? Tasty-looking rod––'

Barney was cut off mid-outrage as, without warning, Bear threw himself towards the two intruders, catching them both off guard.

Barney watched in horror as his best friend was engulfed in a cacophony of hissing, snarling and claws. It was two against one and Barney saw Savannah swipe at Bear's ear as Bart sank his teeth into Bear's tail, causing his friend to yelp and turn, depriving Savannah's outstretched claws of their target.

With an outraged roar, and a silent wail, Barney set off after his friend and was soon himself engulfed in a flurry of fur and claws.

Mid-whack, Barney heard the key in the front door and froze, allowing the unfolded claws of Bart to catch him a stinging blow to his cheek.

'Heeelllllloooooo, boys. It's Mummy. Have you all had a great day?' Katy's voice rang through the house.

Four pairs of eyes bulged as their anger swiftly cooled and they stared at each other in abject horror as Katy walked into the room and surveyed the chaos before her.

Fur littered the dining area carpet and kitchen floor tiles, while each cat sported various cuts, swellings and bruises. Her eyes rested on the hamster cage and she uttered a cry.

'Oh God, where is Sparkle?' she exclaimed as she rushed to pick up the pink palace, placing it gently on the table and re-attaching the tunnel. Ignoring the cats, Katy got on her hands and knees and started to crawl around the kitchen floor.

A small sound made all four cats cock their heads slightly. The faint scrabbling resulted in the small hamster appearing on top of the table, before saluting them and back-flipping through the open door of his cage.

'Oh, there you are,' cried Katy as she stood back up and saw Hank cowering in his wheel. 'Poor Sparkles, have you had a nasty fright from the fighting cats? I'm going to close the door while I deal with this lot and then I will check that you are okay.'

Taking a very loud deep breath, Katy marched to the patio door as the cats watched, unlocked it and flung it open.

'Right, now, get out of my house,' she said.

The four cats registered the anger on the woman's face and after a glance at each other, hung their heads and started to walk, single file to the door.

'Erm, what are you two doing?' said Katy, addressing Bear and Barney while placing her left foot in front of them both to halt their progress. 'Get back inside. Now,' she said to Bart and Savannah, 'you two, well, I suggest you go home and get cleaned up.'

With the door locked behind the departed intruders, Barney released a huge sigh and collapsed onto the floor, while Bear jumped onto the table.

'Hey, Hank. You, okay?' said Bear, keeping a wary eye on Katy as she walked to the sink and opened the cupboard underneath.

'Yeah, I'm good. Bit of a leap but once you two had vacated the room I guessed I'd be safer outside my home than in it.'

'What you jumped?' exclaimed Barney, lifting his head from the floor, clearly horrified. 'But you are so little and you could have been killed.'

'Better than being a plaything for those two.'

'Amen to that,' Bear said, nodding and wincing. 'Ouch! My head hurts.'

'Well, my, my, my whole-body hurts,' complained Barney, 'and let's not forget I saved your ass. Actually, it was your vision as that Savannah creature was gonna nail your eyes––'

'You pair have bigger issues.' Hank's voice cut across the incoming bickering. 'Katy has a bottle, some white fluffy pads and wipes, and you know that shit ain't for my war wounds!'

Bear stood slowly, while Barney shrank back against Hank's cage.

'Come on, boys,' said Katy, advancing across the room. 'Let's get those cuts looked at.'

Hamstergate

Debbie Harrison

'It's gone,' Jane shouted frantically as she ran into the kitchen and halted directly in front of Jake, her pyjama-clad husband, as his spoonful of Weetabix™ hovered mid-air.

His face was perplexed, almost animated, as he tried to understand his wife's previous statement.

'Sorry, what are we talking about?' he asked, a little exasperation in his voice as he continued to deposit the Weetabix into his mouth and began to munch non-plussed.

'The hamster,' she continued, her hands lifting and falling, landing on her hips as she began to pace.

'Hamster, what hamster?'

'Next door, their pet hamster.' Her words blurted out in a rush. Jake looked at his wife, pointing his spoon in her direction.

'That is why you shouldn't agree to look after someone's house at short notice.'

'I don't think Gemma and Tim's family member having a medical emergency was planned. I owed them a favour after the Ann Summers™ package debacle,' she huffed.

Cocking his head slightly, 'Yeah, that was funny.' His chuckle faded quickly as he acknowledged his wife's glare. Clearing his throat, he smirked.

'I hope that taught you that the next time you go shopping for sexy underwear, don't do it online. Apparently, packages can get damaged and then posted to the wrong address; I don't know who was more red-faced, you or Tim, when he came over to deliver the half-open box,' he quipped, trying desperately not to let the ill-contained laughter spill out. Trying and failing miserably. His wife grimaced, which diluted the amusement slightly as he inquired further, 'Okay, so how do you know it's not there?'

'Well, I checked the post for them, then went upstairs to make sure everything was okay, and when I went into little Maxi's room, the cage was sitting in the corner and the metal cage door was open. I looked closer, but there was no sign of the little thing.'

'Did they take it with them?'

'I suppose they could have done, but the food bowl and the water bottle were full, and it looked like fresh bedding had been laid.'

'Just call them and ask.'

'I can't do that; what if they haven't taken the thing with them? I don't want to add another stress for them!' She sighed deeply and blew out a breath. 'What are we going to do?'

'We?' He laughed. 'Oh no, this is all you, don't get me

involved.'

'We're gonna need to search that house,' she announced, ignoring his previous statement. He stood quickly. 'Are you crazy?' His voice rose with every word. 'That's a five-bedroom detached property; that rodent could be anywhere, including inside the walls.'

'There's no need for the dramatics. We might get lucky,' she hissed, grabbing his coffee cup from the kitchen island and taking a mouthful before placing the dirty cup in the sink.

'It'd be quicker going down the local pet shop and buying a new one,' he proposed. 'Err, that could work, but I'm not sure what it looks like!'

Jake shook his head, raising an impressive eyebrow and sighed.

'Let me get this straight.' He paused, collecting his thoughts. 'You suggest that we comb through someone's home looking for something no bigger than the size of my hand, and we have no idea what it looks like?'

She smiled and nodded. 'Uh-huh, so chop-chop, time's wasting. Go get some clothes on!'

A little while later, they stood in Maxi's very pink bedroom.

'God, it looks like Barbie had gastroenteritis when they decorated this room!' Jake exclaimed as he looked around the walls and soft furnishings. Even the pretty duvet-covered canopy bed was pink.

'Shut up, for goodness' sake, and start looking,' she rebuked, her stress levels climbing. 'I'm gonna see if there are any droppings on the floor that I can follow,' she said as she walked towards the cage in the corner and crouched down.

Jake stood in the middle of the room and turned full circle, scratching his head.

'I'm telling ya, this is ridiculous; we're never gonna find it. It could be anywhere. I don't think a bloody hamster can open its cage door and let itself out.'

'I know that, but that's what seems to have happened, so would you please just start looking,' she snapped.

Finding her irritability unamusing, Jake went around the top floor, sticking his head into each room, and judging that the room had been searched, he ventured down the staircase into the expensive-looking kitchen. He noticed and checked the abundance of fruit in the fruit bowl, fingering his way through it, then opened and checked the biscuit tin. No luck!

He was looking in the fridge when Jane walked into the kitchen.

'I know you said that you think a hamster couldn't open its cage door, so, therefore, I think a fridge door would be beyond the realms of capability,' she said, sarcasm riddled through her words.

Jumping at the sudden appearance of his wife, Jake turned with a disparaging look on his face. 'I was checking to make sure there was no food going out of date, and thus, I could dispose of it.'

'Oh, I hadn't even thought of that. They left in such a hurry yesterday they probably overlooked it also.' She smiled. 'Anyway, I think you're right.'

'Always am,' he muttered, his head back in the fridge.

'This is just a long, drawn-out task that will not accomplish our aim,' she announced. He sighed in relief, removed himself from the fridge and looked at his wife.

'So, you're just going to call Gemma and explain what you found.'

'Um, no, you're going down to the pet store to pick up a new hamster,' she explained matter-of-factly.

'I don't think so, anyway, why do I have to go? It's your problem.'

'Jake, you love your wife and always said you'd protect me and even go as far as take a bullet for me.' She spoke in a breathy tone, looking at her husband from under her long lashes as she twiddled with the ends of her long blonde hair, twirling it around her manicured finger while licking her lips. 'Please.'

He stood momentarily, his gaze transfixed, thinking of the many future favours he could command in exchange for this little excursion to the pet store.

'Fine, but if there are any repercussions from this, I will deny any involvement,' he said disapprovingly.

The pet store was just outside town and as soon as he walked in the smell of sawdust hit the back of his throat. Not wanting anyone to see how out of place he felt, he refused to ask for help and meandered aimlessly around.

The store was large with masses of shelving and marketing displays with various animal supplies, which to a non-favouring adult would be seen as an over-indulgence of the epic proportion on the bank account. The further he roamed around the store, the noisier it became. The central display housed large multiple exhibit pens of rabbits, puppies and kittens all waiting for their forever home, according to the sign above the enclosure. The only thing Jake thought was that it would be the local animal shelter when they became a not-just-for- Christmas reject. But he was on a mission, even if he felt his wife had hoodwinked him to do her dirty work, so he sauntered onwards.

Once he had located the cages that housed the sought-after rodents, he quickly got to work trying to decide which one to buy. His first obstacle was which breed to choose. Taking out his phone, he texted his wife.

From: Jake Garfield To: Jane Garfield Date: 1 April 2023 10:35 Subject: Too many breeds

Do you know how many breeds of hamster are available? Which one should I get?

From: Jane Garfield To: Jake Garfield Date: 1 April 2023 10:37 Subject: Too many breeds

Can't you decide? For goodness' sake, tell me what there is.

From: Jake Garfield To: Jane Garfield Date: 1 April 2023 10:39
Subject: I can always come back home – without a hamster

Well, there's a Syrian, it's a sandy colour, more significant than the rest. Then there's a Dwarf Russian, that's grey with dark markings, a lot smaller, and a couple that look more like rats. Their tails are so long.

From: Jane Garfield To: Jake Garfield Date: 1 April 2023 10:40
Subject: Hmmm

Oh wow, I don't think Gemma would allow rats in her house and anything Russian she would disapprove of. The trip last winter to Moscow didn't go well and put her off anything to do with Russia. It was either too expensive or extremely cold; the men seemed rough-and-ready with harsh accents, and the women looked her up and down like she was the plague. Her words, not mine. Probably best to go with the other one.

From: Jake Garfield To: Jane Garfield Date: 1 April 2023 10:41
Subject: What does hmmm mean

You mean the Syrian!

From: Jane Garfield To: Jake Garfield Date: 1 April 2023 10:42
Subject: You're hopeless

Yes! Syria has a warmer climate; she'd probably like that better.

From: Jake Garfield To: Jane Garfield Date: 1 April 2023 10:42
Subject: Indecisions

Are you sure?

From: Jane Garfield To: Jake Garfield Date: 1 April 2023 10:43
Subject: Pulling my hair out

Yes! Just buy a bloody hamster.

An hour later, the new hamster was placed into the cage in Maxi's room and left to settle in. That evening Jane's phone rang.

'Hello,' she began. 'Hi, Jane, it's Gemma.'

'Gemma, hi, how's your dad?'

'He's stable but he had a massive heart attack, so the doctors have him sedated. Tim and I have decided to stick around, but Tim's mum will collect Maxi tomorrow, bring her home and babysit her. I don't want her to miss too much school, and that's the reason I'm calling. I need a little favour.'

'Sure, no problem.'

'Well, it's a little delicate. Could you remove the cage from her bedroom and stick it in the garage out of the way? We'd appreciate it. Tim found Maxi's pet rat, Remy, stiff when he was cleaning out the cage the night before we left to come up here, so we left it there to remove the next day while she was in school, but because we got called away so quickly, we only managed to remove him once the car was packed and Maxi was in her car seat. Luckily,

Tim remembered and disposed of him. We'll tell her the sad news tonight before she comes home tomorrow.'

Houdini

Paul Taylor

The noise woke him. He lay still, ears straining through the darkness. His half-opened eye rested on the red numbers on the digital alarm clock on his wife's side of the bed.

It was 1.50 a.m., both too late and far too early.

The noise was a muffled, intermittent scratching, barely discernible, but there nonetheless and coming from downstairs. His mind wrestled with what it could be. Then an unwelcome dawning,

The hamster! Surely, it hadn't managed to get out of its cage?

He'd no interest in hamsters, really couldn't see the point of them. They slept, ate, scurried about a bit and would often decide to die just for the sake of it. In all, rather tedious creatures. He'd have been more open to the idea of a rat, but his views were dismissed and that afternoon he had found himself trailing behind his wife, Setera, and eight-year-old stepdaughter, Grace, to the pet shop to buy the hamster the little girl had so desperately wanted.

Having acquired the thing, the focus turned to what it should be called. Harry, Horace, Hamish, (they had been assured by the pet shop that it was a male) – or perhaps something not beginning with an 'h', such as Gordon, Quentin or Tedious Ted (his suggestion – and the only one permitted to him during the discussion). The issue was still unresolved by Grace's bedtime.

'Don't worry, darling, it can wait until tomorrow and then you can choose a lovely name for him,' Setera had said soothingly, tucking Grace in for the night.

He too, was now nicely tucked in, snuggled against Setera's soft warm skin, his arm wrapped protectively around her front, feeling the rhythmic beat of her heart and the gentle oscillations of her breathing. He was in her heaven, and yet … he knew he'd got to move and sort this out.

Cursing quietly, he disengaged himself carefully from her and rolled to his side of the bed. Except for the red digits on the clock, the room was pitch black.

It was winter, and cold, as the upstairs of the cottage had no heating. He was naked and he was going to have to find his pyjamas before he left the bedroom. Setera insisted that he wore them when Grace was about, and as usual, he'd kicked off the bottoms once in bed. The top half was on the floor beside him but the bottoms couldn't be retrieved without causing a mini rumpus. Setera was sleeping soundly and he wasn't going to disturb her.

Shivering, he got out of bed, donned the pyjama top and tentatively shuffled and groped his way around the double bed to the door. His senses served him well and he slipped around the partially open door without disturbing her and closed it behind him. The soft glow from the plug-in light was enough for him to make his way down the stairs.

Once at the foot of the stairs he turned left, walked into the lounge, shut the door behind him and turned on the light.

The new cage sat proudly in the middle of the room – two floors and designed with princesses in mind – Grace's decision despite the sex of the hamster – adorned with stairs, toys, and food, was missing the vital piece. The cage door was open and there was no hamster. He recalled that Grace had sat alone with it before she was called for bedtime. She couldn't have fastened the cage door properly. He scoured the room but to no avail. There was no sign of the creature.

He stood still and listened intently. The sound was coming from the kitchen. He turned and mounted the single step to be greeted by a cold, tiled floor beneath his feet. He fumbled along the adjacent wall and managed to find the light switch.

Once again, he listened. Then he got down on all fours and put his face to the ground. His knees ground painfully against the grouted ridges of the cold tiles, as slowly, he rotated, scanning the kitchen floor, as if powered by his phototropic backside.

He saw nothing at first, but he could hear the odd scuffle from underneath the cooker, which was standing three inches from the floor on four spindly metal legs. He tried to peer underneath but was confronted with blackness. Nevertheless, the shuffling continued.

He struggled to his feet and pulled open one of the kitchen

drawers. In it he found a pocket torch he hoped would be there. He switched it on and resumed his position on the kitchen floor, peering under the cooker with the eye nearest the ground. He flashed the torch around. A pair of small white eyes glinted back at him from the inner depths of the cave.

'Okay, I see you, but how the hell am I going to capture you?' he muttered.

He could barely get his arm in the gap between the cooker and the floor, and he would only be able to reach maybe halfway at most, and then with minimal manoeuvrability and next to no vision. Then inspiration struck.

That morning, in preparation for the new arrival, Setera had insisted that he do the vacuuming around the house, something he hated with a passion. He did not like doing it, the sound of it, or the inconvenience caused to him when she was doing it. His feet were invariably in the wrong places and had to be lifted and held two feet from the ground as if performing strenuous stomach muscle exercises. Nevertheless, it seemed now was the perfect time to suspend hostilities towards the activity; well, at least towards the implement itself.

After he had finished that morning's ordeal, he'd put the vacuum cleaner in the utility space, just off a corner of the kitchen. Getting up, he crossed the room and carefully pulled the awkward machine out of its closet, including the four-foot hose attachment.

The vacuum was of the stand-up type, so he carefully positioned it against the wall so as not to obstruct his approach under the cooker. The hose was already attached, which entailed a short wrestling match to straighten the thing out ready for action. He then plugged in the machine, flicked the switch, and with a newly found eagerness for his mission, resumed his position on the floor. He shone the torch underneath the cooker, moving it like a searchlight until it locked onto the two reflecting pin-prick eyes. Taking the hose, he fed it gently towards the target. The hose slithered slowly but surely towards its prey, sucking in the air as if it were a serpentine incarnation of Darth Vader. Then, a tortured, high-pitched squeal, which ended abruptly.

He turned his head sharply, banging and cutting it against the base edge of the cooker as he did so.

'Owwww, bloody hell!' he shouted.

Setera loomed above him framed in the doorway, draped in her negligee, her hand clasped tightly to her mouth.

'Shush, man, you'll wake Grace,' she admonished, switching the vacuum off. 'What on earth are you doing?'

Gradually, and very aware of his naked lower half, he pushed himself to his knees and then into an upright position, the hose of the vacuum following his ascent.

'The bloody hamster escaped,' he spluttered, as he held the hose in front of himself in a misguided attempt to cover his embarrassment.

What had, only a minute or two before, seemed a perfectly rational approach to solving the problem, melted into a pool of humiliation as he tried to explain the situation, kneeling on the floor, half-naked and with blood dribbling from his banged forehead. The protruding four-foot extension intended to preserve at least a modicum of dignity, achieved quite the opposite.

'Well, the hamster escaped and I've been trying to catch it.'

Amidst the commotion, the face of the hamster emerged from beneath the cooker, hesitated, scratched its whiskers, and then scurried out through the kitchen doorway.

If the events of the night had been a traumatic experience for him and Setera, it did not appear to have been so for the hamster as it made its self-assured exit from the kitchen. Setera followed it into the lounge, where it stopped, sat upright, and started munching bits of hamster food that had spilled onto the carpet just outside the open cage door. Having regained her poise, Setera approached it calmly but purposefully, bent down and wrapped her hand around it. She then placed the creature back into its cage, shutting the door behind it. The hamster gazed up at her, seemingly unphased by its nocturnal foray.

By some miracle, Grace had slept through the turmoil. The following morning, she was informed of the previous night's jailbreak, but with many details mercifully, as far as he was concerned, omitted. Instead, he had to suffer towing the party line that he had not fastened the cage door properly and that the hamster had escaped to have a jolly good romp around the kitchen until Mummy had found him and tucked him up back in his cage.

Despite this economy of truth, at least the uncertainty surrounding the choice of name for the new addition to the household had now been resolved. Grace and Setera had decided to call the hamster Houdini. He would call it something else.

Hamsters are Banned in Hawaii
and Other Things to Talk About in the Pub

Katherine Hetzel

'Ere, Frank, did you know that hamsters are banned in Hawaii?

I did not, Terry. What's Hawaii got against the furry little blighters, then?

I dunno. Just summat I 'eard. Thought it might be 'andy to know. For the pub quiz, like.

Ah. One of those useless facts they are so keen to include. Good one. They make nice pets, do hamsters. We've a back garden full of them.

Eh? Thought they lived in cages?

Well, of course they do. But the kids always insist on a funeral every time one of them dies. They only live a couple of years, y'see, so we've had a lot of funerals.

Ah, right. You must know all about hamsters then, Frank. Apart from them being banned in Hawaii.

Apart from that, I suppose I do know quite a few things about hamsters. So ... if you were on Mastermind, would they be your speshi... spechili ...

Specialist subject? Doubt it.

Go on. I bet you know plenty. An' I'm interested.

Are you? Really?

Course I am. And you never know what's going to crop up in the next quiz.

All right, well ... for a start, hamsters are nocturnal, so they only come out at night.

Like the stars.

That's right. They can't see past the end of their noses and get blinded by the sun. They spend all day asleep underground in their burrows, so they don't have to bother looking out for predators like snakes and eagles and the like.

Sounds cushy, Frank. I'd love to spend a day in me bed, keeping out o' the way of everybody.

D'you know, some hamsters even hibernate, Terry. Well, sort of.

Hibernating's what bears do, ain't it? Sleep for months when it gets cold. Would save me hundreds on the heating bill, doing that. 'Ang on, 'ow can you only sort of hibernate? You're either asleep or awake, aren't you?

Well, these sort-of-hibernating hamsters only wake once a week to eat what they've got in their larders, and their heart rate slows from four hundred beats a minute––

Four 'undred beats a minute? That's some serious palpitations, that is.

Whatever you call it, they only have four heartbeats and

two breaths every minute. And they're terribly promiscuous.

They're what, now?

Promiscuous. They ... put it about a bit, you know. The males go looking for the females and when they find one it's wham, bam, thank you ma'am, then off to look for another for exactly the same thing again.

Oh, I get you. I reckon things'd be much easier without the flowers and chocolates and lovey-dovey nonsense y'know. But my Mavis gives me 'ell if I forget any of it when it comes round to our anniversary. Mind, she'd give me 'ell if I even glanced at the barmaid, so I ain't likely to ever get the chance to be promisky wotsit am I?

You know what one of the most interesting facts about hamsters is, Terry? Their teeth never stop growing.

What, never?

Nope. Their incisors, the pointy ones, you know? They keep growing and growing and they have to keep nibbling to keep them short.

Better not tell any science boffs about that then, Frank.

You wh-- Why?

They'll want me as a guinea pig.

What on God's green earth makes you think that?

Well, it's because of me dentures, ain't it? Can you imagine, if they found out what made hamsters teeth grow? They'd want to try growing mine again.

I don't think you need to worry too much about that, Terry. Now, drink up. Last bus home's in ten.

*

Ere, Frank?

Yes, Terry?

You know we were talking about hamsters earlier?

Uh-huh.

You said, they spend most of the day asleep in the dark, so they only come out at night to find their food, yeah?

That's right.

And they've got pointy teeth that keep growing?

Yes. What of it?

Frank ... do you think hamsters are actually vampires?

Author's note:

Hamsters really are banned in Hawaii, because they are originally from a climate similar to that found in the islands and they have a high reproductive rate, which means that in the wild, large colonies of the rodents could jeopardise agriculture and be devastating to the fragile ecosystem.

Mum

Melinda Ingram

Pauline wasn't the Queen of England. She was no Margaret Thatcher. She wasn't famous for anything at all, but she was my mum, and looking back I think she was pretty special. Maybe most people would say that about their mothers; I reckon if you can, you're lucky.

Mum was born in 1933, a child during the Second World War. She might have been a woman of her times, or maybe ahead of her time in some things. Maybe she'd have made a great spy; she was discerning and perceptive, and I know she could keep firm control of her emotions. I only remember seeing her cry once when I was a young child. It was a sunny day mid-1959; we moved to a house at the end of that year when I was four. Our ground floor flat had access to a communal garden where Mum put the clothes through the wringer, turning the big handle on the side before hanging them out. When the line snapped, dumping all her hard work on the scrubby ground, it must have been too much. She was probably exhausted with two young children. I remember being astonished to see her sobbing on Dad's shoulder.

The ensuing years were kind to Mum and Dad, and in many ways, they were fortunate and successful. They made beautiful homes together over the years. They travelled far more extensively than I have done: Japan, South Africa, America, Hong Kong, China, all over Europe. They sailed around Cape Horn. There were adventures and excitement. There were posh dinners and entertainments There were also difficult times, which they shielded us from. I could be angry with her. I could be gobsmacked by her. She was funny, sometimes outrageous, a superb hostess and loyal friend. One quality my mum had in buckets was compassion. She always had an old lady or two whom she had befriended and supported, but this isn't about old ladies, or travel or fortune. This is about her fortitude, bravery and affinity with animals.

My sister rang my mobile on the morning of the 25th of October 2010.

'Mum's had a stroke,' she said. 'We're on the way to the hospital. Can you come?'

Monday was my main teaching day and I was preparing to go to my classroom. I spent half an hour adapting work, so that my mature students could access it with support, and informing people I had to leave. An hour and a half later, I found my brother and sister with Mum, waiting in A&E at Watford. After greetings and hugs all round, and reassurances to Mum who'd smiled a lop-sided smile at me, Ali took my arm.

'Let's get you a coffee after your drive, and some sandwiches. Looks like we'll be here a while.'

As we walked away, she continued, 'It's bad. They want us to sign a DNR.'

'What happened? I didn't ring her yesterday; we were out for the day because of Dave's birthday.'

'We took her some food yesterday morning and she said she was walking to get a paper and she'd have it later. She didn't want to come over in the afternoon. This morning I called in before I went to work. I don't know why, cos I wouldn't normally. It was really hot as I opened the door and the TV was on loud. Mum was sitting on the settee, fully dressed. She'd been there all night unable to call for help. She knew, and I knew straight away what had happened.'

The adrenalin, the need to get there, had kept me going, but now tears sprung to my eyes.

'Poor Mum! I wish I had rung her last night now.'

'You can't think like that, sis. For now, we just have to support her. The staff are saying it would be better if she doesn't survive. She could be completely disabled for ten years or more.'

How prophetic was that! She lived for ten years, dying in 2020 during the pandemic. Not of Covid, no, she gave up when we weren't able to visit her.

Ali and Mike lived close by and shared the visiting so that someone was there every day. I visited every other weekend to give them a break. There were worrying days and better days. On the best ones I would take her for a walk around the grounds in her wheelchair, and then park up somewhere for a chat. I'd read her bits from the paper, and she'd respond with a lifted eyebrow or a grimace or a, 'Well, I think ...' but as soon as she did think the shutters came down and she couldn't share what it was she was going to say. It was so frustrating.

Sometimes she'd shrug and mutter, 'Oh, bollocks!'

I'd think of subjects that I could talk about, memories I knew she'd share. She could listen without pressure. We talked holidays, clothes, food, people, homes we'd lived in. Animals became a favourite. When Mum had been a girl, she'd spent time with her grandparents on their small holding. Collecting eggs from the chickens was something we'd both experienced.

But her dad wasn't sentimental. He would ring a chicken's neck, something I'd never witnessed and never wanted to. During the war she'd been allowed to keep a rabbit. It lived at the bottom of a barrel for want of a cage. Maybe it was never supposed to be a pet, but she thought it was. When they went on holiday – probably to visit relatives – my grandad gave the rabbit to their neighbours, apparently telling them they could 'do what they wanted with it'. When mum went to fetch it back, on her return, they gave her the skin. She must have been broken-hearted.

These stories, for me, were at the beginning of a long catalogue of animals that we'd shared our lives with. Before I was born, Mum had apparently bred Siamese cats and guinea pigs (probably not at the same time) for a while, though how she persuaded her father to allow this I wasn't sure.

'Remember William, Mum? Our little sausage dog?' She smiled. I barely remembered him but I did know what had happened to him. We lived next door to a boys' home. They had a collie, who was agile and used to jump up and down from their coal cellar, which rose about four foot from the ground in the garden. One day, they lifted William up there and he dislocated his back trying to jump down. It rendered him incontinent, which was difficult when my brother was just crawling. He went back to his breeder.

'We had budgies, didn't we?' Most of them lived in a tall cage in the porch outside the front door of our ground floor flat. 'I had one in a cage inside, didn't I mum? He was blue. I think he was called Joey, or was that the green one we had at our next home? I can't remember. We used to let him out to fly around the living room, and settle on our fingers or head. One day he flew through a window we'd forgotten to shut, and that was the end of him!'

Shortly afterwards, my Uncle John, then a teenager, came on his bike and the budgies were packed into a wicker picnic basket and strapped on the back of his bike. I can still see him pedalling down the road with a basket full of our last budgies. Where was he going?

Maybe to a pet shop? Mum's face flickered momentarily, but she couldn't tell me and I'd never asked when she'd been able.

Dave had brought our two border collies outside into the home's large garden for a run. We watched them chasing and retrieving tennis balls, and laughed as Shady overran one and spun round in circles looking for it. As they came nearer to us,

Mum stretched out her left arm – the only limb she could control – and tried to call.

'Come on, come on.' Shady put her head in Mum's lap and Mum caressed her fur with her good hand, her eyes closed.

Once they'd gone in, Dave to make us a cup of tea, I resumed the liturgy. Susie was the first pet I really remembered. I think she was Mum's birthday present just before we moved. I was allowed to name her and I called her after our family friend. Susie was completely black,

and in our new house she took to sitting on the boiler, also black and surrounded by black ceramic tiles, which was recessed into the kitchen wall. The only way you could tell she was there was her shiny eyes if she was awake, or the disappearance of the grout lines in between the tiles. Susie once disappeared for three weeks, and came back nervous, hungry and dishevelled. We never found out where she'd been. I used to love sitting with her curled in my lap, purring and occasionally, needling my legs. In this period, we also had a green budgie and numerous fish, one of which didn't survive my brother Andy trying to stroke it whilst carrying it downstairs to show us all!

'I wanted a dog, though, didn't I, Mum? Do you remember going to get Candy?' I'd saved up my pocket money for weeks because I was going to buy a dog myself if my mean parents wouldn't. I had £1 10s saved when they finally gave in. We went to what must have been a breeder ...

'You wanted us to get a small dog, like a Jack Russell, didn't you? We'd had that poodle come to stay for a week's trial but that didn't work out. Those Jack Russells were so noisy and barky. Once up close, we weren't keen. Then the lady showed us the beagle puppies and we fell in love ... well I did, anyway. I think she cost £10 and I insisted that my money was included in the payment!' I laughed at the memory of what a pain-in-the-neck child I must have been. Candy came home on our laps in the back of the shooting brake car we had then. She turned out to be quite naughty and stubborn, really. She would escape our garden into the woods that surrounded the golf course next door so often we gave up chasing her. She always came back.

'Except one day she managed to "get herself up the duff". That naughty dog had taken to knock over the bins outside the flats opposite our house. She was always looking for food.

Dad went running across the road, alerted by high-pitched dog squealing, to find Candy locked together with a big brown mongrel. She was trying to escape. Dad tried to intervene and got bitten for his troubles. They both had injections, Dad's for tetanus and Candy to stop her conceiving. Good job his worked!'

There was a harrumph from Mum.

'Candy's puppies were lovely though, weren't they? One was born before I went to Brownies, one while I was away. And one after I came home, and that's the one you had to revive. What did you do? Rubbed him with a towel. A little bit of brandy on his tongue ... you blew up his nose, and eventually he breathed and lived. You were so good with them.'

I could appreciate, now, reflecting on my childhood, how amazing she must have been. She was pregnant at the time, and when Ali was born at home a few weeks later, the puppies were in a run outside. Our guinea pigs had had babies too, and we now had over twenty. And we had two rabbits. On top of that, up until just before Ali's birth, we had three foreign students living with us.

'Aww, those guinea pigs, Mum. What about Dougal, eh? Dougal, the longest-lived guinea pig; no ordinary ending for him!'

I knew she was listening, her eyes on mine, as I reminisced. I wanted to breed guinea pigs as Mum had told me she had, and they were easier to keep, the babies being born with hair and quickly independent. We bought a pregnant female who I named Winky because she was blind in one eye. She had short rosetted fur. We also bought a long-haired white male. He was named after the dog from The Magic Roundabout, the children's TV programme that was on every evening at that time. Guinea pigs are very social. They quickly learnt our routines and used to squeak at the tops of their voices when their food was coming. I did an imitation of them, making Mum laugh. Sometimes I bathed them – they could swim well – and blow-dried their hair. I loved those little creatures, and so did she. Once she spent weeks bathing one of the long-haired off-spring with gentian violet every day because a fly had laid eggs in some matted hair and the piggy had a sore full of maggots. Ugh! Guinea pigs usually live for about four to six years, but Dougal was special. He was my first and my last.

'My first, my last, my everything, the answer to all my dreams,' I sang to her, clowning around. She put her hand on my knee. 'Yeah, we both sobbed at the Viking funeral, didn't we?'

Dougal had died the year after I went to college, the last of the guinea pig dynasty. He was at least nine. We'd moved to Hadley just before I went, to a house that was bordered by a brook. Dad said he'd bury him. In the garden, we'd supposed. We were both standing next to each other preparing vegetables for the Sunday dinner, looking out of the large picture window in the kitchen. Dad came past, doing a kind of goose step with Dougal placed on the end of a shovel that Dad was holding out at right angles to his body. He was whistling the funeral march. Mum and I both started crying. As Dad got to the edge to the garden, he flipped the spade in a large arch and launched Dougal's body over the fence and down into the brook. We were incensed; he thought it was hilarious.

We weren't so together at the end of Candy's life. Or maybe we were but I just didn't realise it. I was eighteen, and I'd come home from my first term at teachers' training college in Brighton to have my tonsils out. This was an op. for which I'd been waiting for quite a while because at home I had constant sore throats. Away though, I'd been well. I knew now, years

later, that allergies were the problem. Anyway, I was lying in bed around lunchtime, the day after my op. when Mum came to visit. She had with her the smoked salmon sandwiches I'd requested, tongue-in-cheek, when she'd said I could have anything I fancied. As I unwrapped the delicacies she said, 'Guess what I did this morning?'

'I don't know,' I mumbled through a mouthful of deliciousness, determined to eat them, though I'd only had porridge and ice-cream so far.

'I took Candy to the vet's to have her put to sleep.'

I stared at her for a moment, a high-pitched ringing that sounded a bit like a scream in my ears. I swallowed a ball of nearly chewed brown bread that stuck in my poor throat.

'You did what?'

'She wasn't at all well, Min, she hasn't been for a while. She wasn't going to get better ...'

'You ended her life without telling me, warning me. I can't believe you didn't let me say goodbye!'

I leapt out of bed, furious, raging. I wanted to hit something, hit her. Instead, I turned and ran to the toilet. Locked in, I sobbed. After a few minutes she came in.

'Min, I'm sorry. Come on out.'

I couldn't answer. A few minutes later, a nurse knocked on the door. 'I've got some medicine for you, dear.'

'I don't need any,' I choked out.

'It's best if you do, dear. Please unlock the door.'

I did so. As I followed her back to my bed a porter arrived carrying a very large, beautiful bunch of flowers.

'Miss Narramore? Flowers for you.'

I took them and looked at the card. My emotions swung, in an instant, from complete misery, through amazement, embarrassment, to hilarity. Now I was laughing uncontrollably. Someone at college, who I thought of as a friend, clearly wanted more.

'That nurse wasn't best pleased, Mum, was she? She's booked out a sedative injection for me because you'd told her I was hysterical.'

Mum shrugged her shoulders. Her lip curled with a wry

expression.

'And when I told you, you placed the flowers in a vase some distance from my bed so that my boyfriend wouldn't think they were mine. I hadn't ever experienced such a range of emotions in such a small space of time. It was difficult to deal with. And I know now, though that you were as cut up about Candy as anyone and your way of dealing with things was to keep them "everyday". You'd had a lot of practice in not crying and getting on with things.'

We were holding hands now. I pulled my hand away to give her a sip of her thickened tea from the feeder cup she now had to use. She put her good hand around the cup and I steadied in for her.

'Let's remember some of our other animals, not so sad stories, shall we? What about those naughty hamsters Andy and I had. How did they get out of their cages, anyway? They must have been wooden ones, because they gnawed their way out.'

I put her drink down on the ground next to us and took a big slurp of mine. Mum had lifted her left arm. With her finger pointed she was making a big V gesture, drawing the letter shape repeatedly in the air. I started laughing.

'Oh, Mum! Yes, that's right. We found one of the hamsters at the bottom of Dad's gramophone cupboard where he'd made a nest out of the precious covers from Dad's collection of 78 records, didn't we? But you're right, the other one was standing upright on his back legs in the bottom of a deep vase on the windowsill. He was stuck fast until we tipped it up. What a good job it had been empty.'

We laughed together as we held hands and looked into each other's eyes. This was the first time Mum, Pauline, had been able to show that she was anticipating where a story was going, that she wasn't just reacting, but was right there with me. She was still so sharp in many ways despite having been robbed of her speech in such a cruel way. Would we ever have chosen for her to spend the last ten years of her life incapacitated as she was? No one would, least of all her.

'Take me to Dignitas if I ever go gaga,' she told us on several occasions. But we couldn't once she'd had the stroke so suddenly, because none of the doctors could guarantee she understood and had the capacity to administer the necessary drugs herself. No, we wouldn't have chosen life like this for our vibrant, lively mum, who'd only the week before she was struck down, hosted a family birthday party, having just come back from a trip to Spain with her friends. But you know what? She got on with what life had dealt her with such bravery and humour. I so admired that, though I doubt very much that I'd be the same. The staff all loved her and she made friends. She loved any entertainment and parties. She gave what she could. There were some moments to treasure in those ten years we spent looking after her.

There really were.

Delegated Madness

Stevie Ashurst

Sandbach squeezed himself into a chair at a corner table at Tea Time, a small tea shop in the sleepy seaside village he was visiting. It was clean and had a relaxing atmosphere, but the decor was tired and retro, and not in a deliberate way. This felt like the kind of place Sandbach expected to feel at home, but he didn't.

'How can they run out of tea in a tea shop?' he complained, placing a mug of pale coffee on the table, followed by an oddly shaped nugget of brown and pink. 'And what exactly is rocky road? It's expensive whatever it is.'

Sandbach placed it in the centre of the table, adjusted his chair and leant in close to examine. He prodded the pink marshmallow bits on top before leaning in and sniffing suspiciously.

'Everything all right, dear?' asked the lady cleaning the table next to his. Her name badge said: Diane.

'Oh yes, thank you,' he replied with a smile.

Diane had stopped what she was doing and stared at him, smiling. Sandbach felt uncomfortable. He didn't like attention at the best of times, but especially when he was on holiday.

'I baked those this morning,' she said proudly. 'Well? What do you think?'

Reacting with haste, Sandbach picked up his rocky road and took a delicate nibble from the corner.

'Mmm, lovely,' he replied quickly, far too quickly to have actually tasted anything.

Diane's smile dropped, she opened her mouth to speak but didn't and then walked away looking hurt. A sleepy-looking young woman wearing a tie-dyed t-shirt, leggings and boots put her hand out to get her attention, but Diane just walked past.

'What is wrong with you?' a voice said from under the table. Terrence, his imaginary canine companion, was resting by the table leg. The little terrier pawed at a wooden coffee stirrer. 'You really have a way with people don't you?'

'I don't know what this is,' Sandbach said, prodding his rocky road again. 'I can't give any kind of serious appraisal without understanding all of the properties thoroughly. Diane clearly wanted a response before I was ready to give one. So assuming she was looking for positive feedback, I told her that it tasted good, lovely in fact. How was that wrong?'

Terrence put a paw over his face.

'Is this a cake or biscuit? How can I trust something when I don't even know that basic detail?'

'You're on holiday' Terrence said, 'Stop being a detective

and relax. Who knows, maybe this will become your new favourite thing. And if not, does it actually matter?'

'I suppose not.'

Sandbach took a deep breath then picked up the cake/biscuit thing and took a decent sized bite. It was sweet, crunchy, chewy. Not bad in fact. He raised an eyebrow as he continued to consider the flavour. Hmm, not bad at all. He took another bite and ate it with a level of enjoyment he'd actually not found in a long time. It was delicious. He looked up to see if Diane was still there so that he could give her a genuine response. She finished wiping a table and then carried on into the kitchen area. Tie-dye t-shirt woman got up and put her coat on, peering into the kitchen area before leaving.

'There. What did I say?' said Terrence with some level of satisfaction. 'OK, fair enough, it is pretty good. I'll tell Diane when she comes back.' 'Good.'

Sandbach tucked into the rest of his sweet treat, his enjoyment only reduced each time he took a sip of his hot drink and realised it wasn't tea. As coffee goes, it was really quite bad. The lack of any recognisable flavour didn't seem to improve it.

Terrence's ears pricked up and he wandered further under the table and sniffed at the corner of the wall. Sandbach chose to ignore this and continued eating. Diane walked out of the kitchen with a frown on her face. She looked over in Sandbach's direction and gave a scowl. Sandbach gave a smile and a nod, holding aloft what was left of his rocky road before finishing it off. Diane rolled her eyes then cleared away some cups from the table near the counter.

'That was amazing!' Sandbach exclaimed, as he polished off the last bite. 'I might get another one, if I can get a better drink to go with it.'

There was no answer from below. He peered under the table but Terrence was nowhere to be seen. This was odd for an imaginary companion; one thing you could usually rely on was that a being you create in your mind should be where you expect it to be.

'Terrence? Terrence, where are you?'

Diane was clearing a table nearby and looked up at him. 'Erm, I dropped my ... phone!'

Diane said nothing. Sandbach smiled politely, making a show of waving his mobile phone in the air to signify he had found it.

'Terrence!' Sandbach hissed.

'What?' the little dog replied indignantly. 'What do you mean "what", where were you?'

'I've just met a very interesting character. I think there may be something worth investigating here.'

'I thought you were telling me to relax.'

'Not for you, a case for me,' the dog scoffed. 'Gerald was telling me how this place has a problem with theft.'

'The food is good but I wouldn't--' 'Not the food, money is going missing.'

Sandbach sat back and thought for a moment. He really didn't want to get involved but as always, he was intrigued.

'Who is Gerald?' 'Gerald is a hamster.'

'Of course he is. Can I talk to him?' 'No.'

'Is he uncomfortable talking to police?' 'I don't think so.'

'Then why not?'

'He is my imaginary companion.'

Sandbach opened his mouth then closed it again. 'OK, since when? How long's this been going on?'

'Since always. I assumed you knew,' Terrence said, cocking his head to one side. 'Is Gerald here now? Can I see him?'

'Yes, he's here, but no, you can't see him.'

'Then why would I know you had an imaginary hamster called Gerald?'

'Because I'm a figment of your imagination, which means that I, and therefore Gerald, are constructs of your bizarre mind.'

'Fair point.'

Terrence scratched himself with his back leg then looked expectantly at Sandbach. 'Can I continue?' Terrence asked, sounding slightly annoyed.

'Of course, please do.'

Terrence hopped up onto the chair opposite, which Sandbach appreciated. It meant he could stop staring under the table.

'Gerald believes something isn't quite right with this place. Not everything is as it seems.'

'He sounds a very astute for a hamster. And what's leading him to this conclusion? I couldn't comment on whether Diane is fiddling her taxes, but her baking seems fine to me.' 'The clientele are a little unusual for a coastal tea shop don't you think?' Terrence said quietly, nodding in the direction of several youths in the far corner, all on mobile phones while idly munching their pieces of rocky road.

Sandbach felt a little foolish at not having spotted this sooner. He was more used to life in the city, so suspicious-looking youths were part of the everyday decor. But in a sleepy seaside town it did seem a little odd.

'I don't know the residents in this area, but if the town isn't full of smiling pensioners then they can't populate the tea shops,' Sandbach replied. 'Perhaps this is the liveliest place to hang out in the area. A bizarre thought, but it could be true. Besides, this stuff is very good. I had my doubts but I think I might get some more.'

With that Sandbach got up and wandered over to the counter. The four youths stopped talking and stared at him. He turned his attention back to the counter. There was a small selection of sad and tired looking cakes and biscuits on display that he hadn't spotted before, perhaps because they were tucked away to one side. They looked quite stale and dry and he could swear one of the cakes had mould on it, whereas the bizarrely huge quantity of rocky road, looked delicious. Clearly, this must have swayed his decision originally and he felt drawn to it again, despite the high price.

Diane came to the till, looked at Sandbach and raised an eyebrow. 'Yes?'

'I'll have another piece of your delicious rocky road please.' Diane's face lit up and she beamed with pleasure.

'Of course, dear, and another coffee?'

'Erm no, thank you. Just the rocky road please.'

She nodded, placed another piece onto a small plate, then put it on the counter. 'Six pounds fifty please.'

'So, how come this rocky road is so much more expensive than the other cakes?' Diane looked a little confused. 'Do you want it or not?'

'Oh yes, I definitely want it, I just wondered whether it was a special recipe.'

'Absolutely, dear, old family recipe,' she said with a smile and a wink.

Sandbach paid and walked back to his seat, glancing at the youths sitting in the corner. He nodded to them to signify that he had no intention of causing them any problems. One of group – a large and imposing figure wearing a bright yellow hoodie and smiling with gold teeth – nodded back to him. He didn't smile, or wave, or do anything visibly nice like that, but a nod from someone like this was practically like running over and giving him a hug. Not something he'd expected. Sandbach sat down feeling quite unnerved by the situation. He was used to verbal abuse, laughter at his expense, and on a good day, scornful looks, but never what he could only interpret as a low-level mark of respect. Perhaps the youth had been looking at Diane, or someone else who had come in. There was no one else near the counter. He glanced casually back at the youths, and sure enough, the one in the yellow hoodie was still looking at him. He nodded again and then turned back to conversation with his companions. The nod was definitely for him.

'Made a new friend?' Terrence asked with amusement.

'Possibly, and that worries me,' Sandbach replied.

'Maybe they're all on holiday too, enjoying the local scenery and tea shops.' Sandbach glared at Terrence.

'Or maybe,' Terrence continued, 'they're here for something else.'

'Yes, but what?'

Sandbach sat back and pondered the matter, before his stomach reminded him that his portion of rocky road was being neglected.

'I'm seeing familiar signs in this place,' Sandbach mused. 'People who don't fit in their surroundings, a business that shouldn't work but clearly does, in a location that has no right to be this popular.'

'Absolutely,' Terrence replied, nodding enthusiastically. 'Are you thinking what I'm thinking?'

'I think so ... it has to be a cult.'

'What? You're definitely not thinking what I'm thinking,' Terrence said, sitting back in astonishment. 'Why would you even say that?'

'Think about it ...' Sandbach paused to take an enthusiastic bite from his chocolatey treat. 'These people are drawn together by a common purpose ... oh this rocky road is so good.'

'Concentrate,' Terrence said, banging a paw on the table.

'Sorry. This place is probably their initial meeting point, somewhere to show they're committed, to inform some kind of leader that they're committed, which has to mean their actual key location is nearby, and that someone important is representing them here or watching them perhaps.

'Which means ... yes, that's it! Which means the youth in the yellow hoodie doesn't know who the representative is, and therefore nodded to me to show their respect, in case they think I could be the one watching them.'

'No! Just ... no,' Terrence said firmly. 'Seriously, what's wrong with you? You've dealt with so many messed-up and bizarre cases that you can't see the glaringly obvious ones anymore.'

'OK then, Scooby-Doo, what do you think it is?'

'Drugs! It's clearly drugs.'

Sandbach pondered the idea and shrugged.

'It's possible I suppose, but not everything's about drugs you know. Sometimes things happen that don't come back to drugs. Remember that library a couple of years ago?'

Terrence gave a visible shudder. 'Just call it in and let the local force deal with it.'

'And if it's something else, something deeper? They'll miss it or at least mess it up. The cult will scatter and then we've blown any chance of catching them.'

Sandbach took the opportunity to better inspect the customers in the cafe: the youths still at their table at the far end, there was elderly couple in matching blue rain jackets, talking quietly near the counter and there were two middle-aged men in deep but hushed conversation at a table near the middle of the cafe, dressed as though they had been hiking. Then just as he glanced at the door, three elderly women walked in talking in very animated voices – something had clearly upset them outside. One of them was wearing a bright pink coat and seemed very angry indeed. They congregated by the till where Diane joined the conversation.

'Well they don't look like your typical drug dealers,' Sandbach said.

'Not everyone has to be involved. And anyway, they certainly don't look like they're part of a cult,' Terrence said, getting annoyed. 'Just call it in.'

Sandbach shook his head, picked up his phone, typed a message and then put it back in his pocket.

'They'll pick it up and head over at some point. I don't imagine this will be high priority, so maybe later today. In the meantime, I can look for evidence of a cult.'

Sandbach gave Terrence a knowing nod. Terrence rolled his eyes.

'From what Gerald told me, you might want to look in the kitchen first,' Terrence said. 'It's not drugs,' Sandbach replied flatly. 'But I'll take a look.'

Sandbach walked back to the till for a third time, nodding at the youths in the corner, but they were too deep in their own conversation to notice. One of the hikers looked up at him and smiled. Sandbach smiled back. He was about to walk past then an idea struck him.

'I'm sorry, you don't know where the toilet is do you?'

'Yes, it's just by door,' the hiker replied. 'Just pop through that little door on the right, there's a bit of a corridor then it's the room at the end with a sign. You can't miss it.'

The hiker stood up and pointed in the right direction, but then remained standing and smiling at him just a little too long, which was slightly awkward.

'Thank you, much appreciated,' Sandbach replied before shuffling away.

He couldn't head into the kitchen now that he'd been shown where to go, but it did give him opportunity to look around a bit more without raising suspicion. The old lady with the purple rinse and beige anorak had just gone through the door, so he followed her into the corridor.

'Won't be long dear,' the old lady said over her shoulder, 'but I've got to go.'

'Not a problem,' Sandbach called out as she shut the door quickly behind her. He thought he'd heard someone call her Doris earlier.

It was a very small corridor, not much space for a queue if they had one. There was just a view of the carpark through net curtains to the left, but there was a door on the right and there was no sign, or notice, to say what it was, or to keep out. Sandbach put his ear to it and listened. Nothing. He twisted the round metal door knob and peeked in. It was a small office with no windows and no lights. Perhaps part of another room initially but walled off. He flicked the switch on the wall and stepped carefully inside, pulling the door shut behind him. There was an old yellowing computer on the desk to the right that looked as if it hadn't been used in a long time, which Sandbach was relieved to see – he hated computers. The boxes of papers on top, and no visible keyboard or mouse, were the biggest clue to this. To the left there were shelves packed with books, folders and files, with sheets of paper jammed in between everything. This would take days to examine. He decided something was better than nothing. Recent information was usually right there on top so might be the biggest giveaway.

The first thing he saw on top of the boxes was a recipe. It didn't look complicated but had an odd title – Primo Choco.

Sandbach tucked it under his arm and started riffling through the first box on top. There were some old cookbooks, which looked as if they'd come from a car boot sale or charity shop; nothing special. The next box seemed fairly heavy and it rattled, but after opening it carefully, he found it just had broken crockery in. Sandbach moved to the shelves on the right-hand side to see if there was anything on them. Chest height, right in front of him, seemed the logical place to look first, so he did, but there were just receipts for food and drink from five years ago. Nothing out of the ordinary, or even current.

The sound of the toilet flushing made him hold still for a moment. He could hear slow footsteps in the corridor. He waited until these had passed before he carried on looking, but almost immediately the door behind him opened.

'Diane, I saw the light on under the door, be careful, dear-'

The old lady with the purple rinse – who might be called Doris – stopped talking when she saw Sandbach. She stared at him for a few moments before speaking.

'What are you doing in here?' she asked.

The old lady spoke with a slightly shaky but unnervingly calm voice.

'So sorry, I thought this might be another loo?' Sandbach chuckled, but stopped when Doris didn't laugh, or even smile.

'Is that so?' She stepped into the room and shut the door behind her. 'And who might you be?'

'When I'm not stuffing my face I try to solve crimes,' Sandbach said in his best reassuring voice.

'Oh dear,' she said, as she started walking towards him.

'I'm serious, I'm a detective. My badge is in my coat.'

'Oh, I believe you, it's just a shame you wandered in here.'

Doris reached into her tan coloured handbag and pulled out black-handled flick-knife. She released the mechanism deftly and raised it towards Sandbach without blinking.

'It's going to be one of those holidays isn't it?' Sandbach said to himself, placing the folder on top of the boxes to his side and stuffing the paper into his pocket.

'What was that?'

'You're part of this whole operation too, aren't you?' Sandbach said.

'Better believe it, bitch. I'm the muscle,' she replied. 'And you're just too nosey.'

She lunged at Sandbach, who instinctively grabbed the folder again just as the knife blade appeared through the other side, missing his eyes by millimetres. Sandbach yanked it to one side, pulling the knife out of her hands, before he threw it behind him and out of her reach.

She grabbed the bag again, and this time pulled out a small pistol, and proceeded to attach a silencer to the end.

'Be a good boy and stay still will you?' she said, as if she was talking to a toddler who'd grazed a knee.

Sandbach dived behind the computer desk and pulled the stack of boxes over behind him. There were a couple of quiet-ish bangs and tiny bits of cardboard and paper flew up in front of him. Sandbach grabbed the box of broken crockery and threw it in her direction. Doris swore as it knocked her backwards. She recovered herself then stepped over the box and lined up the gun with his head. Click. Click, click, click.

Doris dropped the gun and this time pulled out two sets of brass knuckles. She dropped the bag and slipped them on, before beating her fists together with a metallic thud.

'You've got to be kidding,' Sandbach exclaimed.

She raised her fists and started bobbing and weaving towards Sandbach.

Sandbach grabbed the small, but heavy, CRT computer screen. In a fit of frustration and panic, he threw it at the old woman. She skilfully darted sideways, but as Sandbach had a terrible aim, she accidentally moved into the path of the flying monitor. It caught her square in the chest and sent her flying backwards into the wall opposite. She gave a small groan, indicating she was still conscious, but she didn't get up.

The door opened again. Sandbach grabbed a dusty keyboard he could now see and raised it menacingly above his head.

'Detective Inspector Sandbarge?' a uniformed policeman with a very deep voice asked. 'Sure, why not?' Sandbach replied with relief as he placed the keyboard back down. 'We got a message from you. Someone was in the area and called in. There was a minor kerfuffle, backup was called in and ... well, we think we've caught the whole operation.'

'I've only been in here a few minutes!' Sandbach exclaimed. 'You can't have wrapped up an entire cult network in a few minutes.'

'Sir?'

Another figure peered inside the door. It was the familiar and self-satisfied face of Detective Inspector Susan Roper in her immaculate trouser suit and high heels.

'Sandbag, we need you to give a statement––' She looked down at the old woman with the purple rinse who was slumped against the wall with a computer monitor on her lap. 'What happened here? Came at you with a knife did she?'

'Well actually––'

'Remind me not to book you for Care in the Community.'

Sandbach followed her out of the room and into the main cafe. It was swarming with police. The gang of youths were all cuffed and bent over the table. The hikers were being physically restrained and the elderly couple were being questioned.

'My goodness, all of them in on it?' Sandbach asked.

'Oh yes, this could be a huge operation. And this lot appear to be the ring leaders.'

'Seriously? Even the elderly couple?'

'Actually, we think they might just be tourists, but not ruling anything out yet.'

'So how many people are part of the cult then?'

DI Roper looked at him sideways. 'Cult?'

Sandbach saw Terrence sitting at the table looking very smug. Then he looked back at Roper.

'It's drugs, isn't it?'

'Yes, of course it's drugs,' she replied. 'Excuse me, grab a seat and someone will be over in a minute. We're trying to find details of what's in it.'

Sandbach sat down opposite Terrence. His cold excuse for coffee was still there, so he took a sip and finished off the last few crumbs of his rocky road.

'So, what was it?' Sandbach asked. 'Coke, amphetamines,

heroine, what?'

'Cannabis,' Terrence replied.

'Seriously? I didn't see anyone smoking.'

'Oh, they weren't smoking it,' Terrence said with a huge grin on his face. Sandbach looked down at the small plate in front of him.

'No. Oh for goodness' sake!'

'That's right – you've eaten half the evidence.'

It then dawned on him what he'd stuffed in his pocket earlier. He pulled out the screwed-up piece of paper with what he now assumed was the secret recipe for the rocky road he'd just polished off.

'I need a holiday,' he exclaimed. 'Without sarcastic dogs or mysterious hamsters.'

Dead on Arrival

Peter Rogers

For Tommy, Mr Frisky was everything. He would feed him, give him water and much to his mam's surprise, even clean up after him.

Best of all for Tommy was watching Mr Frisky race around the carpet in his plastic ball, with a close second being when his pet hamster got up a head of steam on the wheel in his cage. Mr Frisky was Tommy's best friend in the whole world.

It was a daily routine that every day, after school, Tommy would gently place Mr Frisky into his ball and spend the next hour pursuing the hamster throughout the house.

But today was different.

Tommy dropped his school bag and ran into the bedroom.

'Maths was hard, science harder, but history was cool. We learnt all about the Egyptians.'

Tommy liked to inform Mr Frisky of his day's activities.

'Did you know the Egyptians built pyramids, worshipped

cats and wrapped their dead in bandages and called them mummies?'

Mr Frisky said nothing.

Tommy found the ball and split it open.

'They lived by the Nile and had lots of gods too,' Tommy continued as he opened the hamster's cage.

'Mr Frisky?'

There was no movement from inside the cage.

Tommy poked the pile of wood shavings in the corner.

'Maaaaammmmm.'

Mam explained that Mr Frisky was quite old and that at least he hadn't suffered. 'I'm doing enough suffering for the both of us,' wailed Tommy.

'We could get another one,' offered Mam.

'No, Mam,' protested Tommy. 'There will never be another Mr Frisky.' 'Well at least we can bury him by the goldfish,' said Mam.

'No way,' spluttered Tommy indignantly. 'No worm is making a meal of Mr Frisky.' 'But Tommy.'

'No buts, there's got to be another way.'

The other way was discovered in the Yellow Pages – taxidermists. There was one in town, it was called Dead on Arrival.

Mr Frisky was wrapped in a clean sports sock that gave the resemblance of a shroud and loving placed in a shoebox. The short car journey was taken in revered silence. A request from Mam for some music to lighten the trip was countered with a deep serious stare and shake of the head from Tommy.

The inside of the shop was enough to give you nightmares. Sightless eyes bored down from every shelf and followed their steps to the shop counter. Tommy instinctively pushed himself into his mam's side and she too felt the benefit of her son's contact.

A set of beaded curtains that hung over a doorway behind the counter spread open and a young man appeared through them.

'Good afternoon, madam.' He turned to Tommy. 'Young sir. How can I be of assistance?'

Tommy solemnly laid the shoe box on the counter and removed the lid.

'Poor little fellow.' The shop assistant touched the bridge of his glasses then picked up the sock and removed the hamster. He stroked the fur.

'Can you do, what you do, so I don't have to put him in the ground, ever?' asked Tommy.

'Of course I can,' replied the man. 'I will have him ready by the weekend.'

Tommy was so excited. He just couldn't wait for the weekend. It was going to be like Christmas and birthday all wrapped up as one. Mr Frisky was coming home.

'You do know it won't be the same,' said Mam. She was becoming concerned when she had seen Tommy clean out the cage and put in fresh wood shavings. He had also washed Mr Frisky's plastic ball. She rang up the taxidermist and explained her problem.

'Could you do anything that would make it look alive?' she

enquired.

'I was thinking of mounting it on its back legs with the water bottle in its mouth,' said the taxidermist.

'Is there no way of making it move? You know, stick wheels on it and put a motor inside.'

'Can you do that?' asked the shop owner.

'I don't know. You're the one who stuffs animals for a living.'

'Not really, Mr Frisky will be my first job. I only took over the business last week from my uncle.'

Mam sighed. 'Well just do what you can please.'

The shop owner put down the phone and stared at the hamster. He was quite happy with the work he had done so far. He had washed the fur, dried it and gave it a nice brush. However, he had not got round to the skinning bit, nor the spooning out of the inners, and as for the popping out of the eyes and replacing them with glass ones, errgh. The eyes, he didn't even like the idea of touching his own, hence the glasses, no contact lenses for him.

He picked up a large tome entitled, Taxidermy Made Easy, as he did, he noticed a piece of paper sticking out of the back. The paper was really old, in fact it didn't feel like paper and the writing on it was something similar to hieroglyphics. He couldn't make any sense of it except the letters PTO written in biro on the bottom right of the parchment. On the other side there was an English translation and it may just offer a potential solution.

The ancient art of reanimation was explained in precise

detail and seemed quite simple; you just inject the corpse with cat blood. But this wasn't any old cat blood, this blood had to be extracted from the immortal sac located behind the left ear of the sacred Egyptian cat. The manuscript explained that this was where the nine lives of a cat could be found. Kittens were the best source because you could milk four or five lives and still leave enough for the kitten to have a reasonable long life with the remaining ones. Unfortunately, the practice had caused the extinction of the sacred cat and only a few samples of the precious elixir were still in existence.

It just so happened that there was a phial with the moniker Feline Extraction, in the drawer, next to some syringes. He had seen them before and had thought nothing of them.

Gingerly, he started to pour the watery red liquid into one of the syringes when a rogue glass eye inexplicably rolled across the tabletop. The shock was so great that he dropped the container. It smashed on the hard floor. Its contents seeped away in the cracks in the tiles.

He looked at the small quantity he had successful transferred to the syringe. It would have to do.

Carefully, he picked up the hamster corpse in one hand and the syringe in the other. After reading the instructions one more time, he estimated where the base of Mr Frisky's skull was and thrust the needle deep into the brain.

Pushing down the plunger, he released the life-giving fluid into the hamster.

Almost immediately the stiffness of the rigor mortis disappeared and Mr Frisky stretched as if waking from a deep sleep and commenced with some much need grooming.

The amazed taxidermist placed the little Lazarus into a cage.

The next day, Tommy and his mam entered the shop. She looked at the shop owner with narrow quizzical eyes that widened to saucers and beyond when Mr Frisky was revealed sitting in the corner of the cage, very much alive, still busily grooming himself.

There was no explanation the taxidermist had to offer, and no charge for this, his miracle. The delight on Tommy's face was payment enough and as he had used up all the cat lives, it wasn't something he could do again.

After Tommy and his mam had left, the taxidermist checked the rest of the rules of reanimation. To his horror, it stated at the bottom in handwriting more akin to the fine print on a contract, DO NOT EXCEED THE MAXIMUM DOSAGE OF ONE DROPLET.

'One droplet!' he said out loud to his stuffed collection. 'There was enough in that syringe for a hundred and one droplets. What have I done?'

Later that day, during dinner, Mam asked Tommy how Mr Frisky was.

Tommy looked at her with a sad face.

'He won't go into his plastic ball any more, or play in his wheel. All he wants to do is sleep or groom himself. I've seen him play with a piece of string and he even tried to drink some of my milk. But weirdest of all, I'm sure he's purring.'

Teacher's Pet

Hilary Smith

In the staffroom they tried to put me off with stories about escapees stuck in air vents, or floating in the boys' toilets, or returning after the school holidays a different size or colour.

'Certainly wouldn't risk it with a McCready in the class!' They said. I'm undeterred. That lot haven't tried anything new in years.

Looking around at my class of four-year-olds, I see the usual character mix of cute and cruel, disarming and delightful, in their upturned faces.

I place the cage in the middle of the carpet.

'Who might live here?' I say. The children get up on their haunches, elbowing each other out of the way to get a better view. Even Harvey lifts his badly shorn, scabbed head.

'Thnake,' says Mia, confidently unaware of her lisp. I must follow up that speech therapy referral.

'Our Ben's got a snake,' mumbles Harvey. His head is down

again, fiddling with the Velcro on his trainers. 'An' a tranchla.'

A few squeals and worried faces.

'No, not a snake, or a tarantula, but thank you, Harvey.' Please don't sabotage it before I've even got started.

'It's small and furry. Come on, everyone, put your thinking caps on.' Excited voices call out:

'Kitten?'

'Rabbit?' 'Chicken!'

Harvey murmurs, 'It's a bleedin' 'amster.'

I should tell you off for swearing but ...

'Well done, Harvey! That's right.'

I open the cage and move the bedding aside to reveal a young hamster curled into a tight ball. I lift its fragile, sleepy form and with only a little trepidation, begin the risky process of handing it to each child in turn. I know what I'm doing ... it's going to be ok.

Shane, Courtney and Mia all handle the hamster with varying degrees of gentleness, as do Tom and Samira. Then it's Harvey's turn. Deep breath.

Taking the tiny creature from Samira, I place it in Harvey's filthy outstretched hands, cradling my own around them. His eyes widen, blink, soften as he holds the furry ball. He's being so tender ... this is going to work!

With slow, infinite care, I remove my hands. 'You've got him,' I say in a whisper.

'Miss!' Courtney's voice pierces the quiet concentration. 'Shane hit me!' I turn around, breaking my attention on Harvey for a second. That's all it takes.

When I look back it's too late. Harvey opens his fisted

hand, grinning at me, and drops the tiny corpse at my feet. Then he bolts out of the classroom.

Shit. Shit. Shit.

'Harvey McCready! Get back here!' I yell down the corridor. But it's no use, he's gone and I'm left with a dead hamster and a class of distressed children.

A few years later, a bright young newly qualified teacher is in the staffroom, telling us she's thinking of hatching some chicks in her classroom. I say nothing. Harvey's younger brother is in that class.

She'll learn. She'll learn.

The Houdini Hamster
The Great Escape

Malcolm Welshman

I was somewhat alarmed when Josh Higgins, one of the neighbours down the road from us, appeared on the back doorstep of our cottage, Willow Wren, with his eleven-year-old son in tow, carrying a hamster cage.

'We've brought round Odysseus,' said Josh.

I felt my eyebrows crease together in puzzlement.

'He's a Greek god,' said his son, Eddie. 'Homer wrote about him in The Odyssey.'

'Eddie's into Greek mythology at the moment,' explained Josh, as if that would allow my eyebrows to unknot. It was not the name that was puzzling me but why the rodent was here in the first place.

My wife provided the answer.

'Hi, Josh, Eddie,' said Maxeen, materialising at my shoulder.

'So, this is our holidaying hamster is it?' She took the cage being proffered by the boy.

'Odysseus,' he said. 'It means he likes giving pain.'

Once the two of them had left, Maxeen filled me in as I gazed into the hamster cage now deposited on the kitchen breakfast bar. Seems she'd bumped into Josh while in Ashton's Post Office and he'd asked the favour of her. Could we look after Odysseus for the week while they were away for the half-term?

'You didn't think to ask me?' I queried.

'Sorry, dear. I didn't think you'd mind. They seemed to be in a bit of a fix. So, I said it wouldn't be a problem.' She looked at me. 'Well, it's not, is it?'

'Could be if he escapes. You know what my track record with hamsters is like.'

It did seem that many of my encounters with these furry fellows and their rodent cousins ended up with them escaping, as if they sensed I was a bit cack-handed. 'Hey ho … I'll give him the slip' way of thinking as soon as the cage door was opened. Certainly, some hamsters seemed very apt at slipping out of their cages, as if cunningly planned. The POWs of Stalag Luft 111 may well have been famous for their tunnelling techniques but paled into insignificance with the likes of these rodents. When in my hands – or more often than not, out of them – they had many 'Great Escapes'.

'All I can say is that if he does decide to go on his own odyssey, heaven help us if it's an epic one,' I went on. How prophetic those words turned out to be. Homer would have been delighted.

Odysseus didn't make an appearance until early evening, emerging from his nest of shredded paper towelling to sniff the air with a twitch of his snout, his button-black eyes gleaming – no doubt sizing up his escape routes. I had been expecting him to be of the standard golden variety, honey-coloured coat with white undercarriage. But as he tucked into a bowlful of mixed grain and sunflower seeds topped with a sprinkling of peanuts – Eddie had provided a very comprehensive menu for Odysseus to savour – I found myself watching a very smart-looking rodent with rich mahogany-red fur over-ticked with black guard hairs; coat colouring that would blend very nicely with our carpet should he ever seize the opportunity to trek across it.

There was no sign of him the next day. I wasn't concerned. Hamsters are nocturnal, sleeping during daylight hours.

'No Odysseus then?' I remarked glancing at my watch as Maxeen and I sat down for our supper. Just gone seven o'clock. Meal finished, another glance at the cage. Still no appearance. All rather ominous. Surely Odysseus should be feeling hungry by now? Best take a look. Open cage door. Notice clip on door loose. Rising panic. Prod nest. Empty. Bugger, the sod's got out. Search party time. I gazed around the living room, the endless hidey-holes from down the backs of the two settees to the hamster-sized gaps in the uneven skirting boards. And in true heroic expeditionary-style, Odysseus could already have mountaineered up the stairs to immerse himself in the subterranean depths of the overhead floorboards.

Great.

All the while, Queenie, the cat we owned, looked on with a nonchalance that suggested she couldn't give a toss; and our two recently acquired rescue dogs, Judy and Winnie, having had their supper, were in full-bellied bliss stretched out asleep in front of the fire.

'Could be anywhere,' said Maxeen, in what I considered to be a very unhelpful observation. But anywhere had to be somewhere. And we felt an obligation to at least mount a search party in an attempt to find him. Maxeen's head went under one settee. Nothing.

Mine went under the other. No trace. Kitchen cupboards opened and closed without the slightest stirrings from within. Not the twitch of a whisker.

'I'll leave the cage door open and a bowl of food inside,' I said when eventually we decided to abandon the search and get some shut-eye ourselves.

The bowl was empty the next morning. Maybe there might be a curled-up Odysseus, fast asleep in his nest. I poked around inside it, hoping I might prod a warm furry body. But nope, nothing. An empty nest. Odysseus had obviously chosen to slumber elsewhere.

'Well, he's taken the food,' I said, 'so at least he must be around somewhere.'

'It might have been mice,' said Maxeen. Thanks, dear, that's cheered me up no end.

'I heard of one hamster that disappeared for three months,' she went on. 'And?'

'It was eventually found nesting in the vacuum cleaner.'

I wasn't sure of the point Maxeen was making, but I did

check the Hoover bag later that morning and riffled through the recycle bins. Just a load of rubbish. No hamster.

But my wife hadn't finished. 'There was also that case of a hamster that wasn't found until the people moved house. It then emerged from a pot plant. Apparently, it had burrowed down into it.'

I gazed around the living room at the seven potted plants we had in there. Add to them, the cluster of pots in the hall and several more lining the windowsill in the kitchen and that equated to a sizeable number of pots where Odysseus could have gone to ground. No way was I going to root through that lot on the remote chance I could unearth him. I'd go potty in the process.

'Tell you what,' I said, 'let's see if the Internet has any suggestions on how to recapture a hamster.' So, I Googled 'fugitive hamsters' and was presented with several options.

The first one involved encircling a bowl of food with a fine dusting of flour. The next morning you were to study the area and pick up the trail of tiny floury paw prints, which would lead you to your escapee's hidey-hole.

It worked in as much we did indeed find floury footprints. Masses of them, all over the floured floor. Odysseus may well have spent a night on the tiles but it seemed the mice did as well – they'd had a ball and done a conga around the bowl without any sense of direction as to where they were eventually heading off to.

Another suggestion was to place the food bowl on a large sheet of tissue paper and then lay in wait with the lights off until you heard the tiny patter of feet rustling on the tissue.

Then you pounced. I did as instructed, turned the lights off, and fell asleep.

By the third day, with Odysseus still at large, we were beginning to panic. Eddie and family were due back in three days' time. How could we face them with an empty hamster cage and tell them that Odysseus was missing presumed ... well just what was presumed? That one of our dogs or cat may have eaten the hamster? We didn't have the stomach for that even if our pets did.

Maxeen came up with the idea of a bucket trap.

'We make a staircase of books to the top of a plastic bucket with some food lying in the bottom of it and entice Odysseus up the books by placing a sunflower seed on each step.

He'll get to the top, see the food inside and jump in. But then find he can't jump out again.'

I was dubious. And was proved right. The trail of sunflower seeds up the books was left untouched. As did a trail of peanuts and sweet corn I then tried.

Undaunted, Maxeen found another Internet idea.

'We tie some string to a monkey nut. Odysseus will pick up the nut and return to his hiding place, leaving the string trailing behind him.'

Odysseus did find the monkey nut with twine attached to it, but decided to crack open the shell and eat the nuts inside there and then. Outwitted yet again. Talk about stringing us along.

I came up with another inspired plan. Two pieces of string taped to either side of Odysseus's food bowl. Tie the other two ends to the top door of his cage so the bowl dangles down rather like a trapeze. Prop the door open with a match stick. In pops Odysseus, jumping down into the bowl. His weight forces the door to snap shut. Ta ... ra – we've got him.

'What do you think of my cunning plan?' I asked Maxeen.

'Not a lot.'

Nor did Odysseus by the look of the empty cage, door still ajar, food bowl untouched, which I discovered the following morning.

Odysseus was due to be collected by Josh and Eddie later that afternoon. So, it looked as if we were going to have own up to being poor custodians of their pet. Miserable failures in fact. Homer would have thoroughly disapproved.

I spent the rest of the morning digging over the vegetable patch in preparation for some spring planting of onion sets and seed potatoes. At least it was a distraction from worrying about missing rodents. It had just gone midday when I heard our spaniel, Judy, barking indoors. A furious series of excited yaps. Then silence.

I had a sudden thought. Ahrr ... she's spotted Odysseus. I gulped imagining Judy doing the same as a hamster slid down her throat. I dropped my spade and raced up the garden path just as Judy came bounding out of the back door, tail wagging in a frenzy of excitement. She headed straight towards me down the path and as we met, she stopped and looked at me, Odysseus hanging from her jaws. I immediately dropped to my knees and extended my left arm towards her hand, palm up.

'Good girl,' I murmured, 'what a good girl.'

Judy gave a little grizzle, sidled up to my hand and dropped

Odysseus in it. He immediately made to spring up and jump.

'Oh no you don't, matey,' I declared clamping my right hand over him, cocooning him between my palms. 'You're not going anywhere other than back in your cage. Your wanderings are well and truly over.'

When Josh and Eddie turned up later that afternoon, the first question Eddie asked was: 'Is Odysseus okay?'

'Fine, yes,' I replied.

'Did you manage to let him out at all?' 'Well, actually--'

Maxeen butted in: 'He had the run of the place every day, didn't he, dear?' she said looking up at me.

'Er ... yes, definitely.' I nodded enthusiastically.

'Please to hear that,' said Josh. 'We didn't like the thought of him being cooped up all the time. Though of course it could have been a bit risky letting him out. But I'm sure you didn't let your cat or dogs anywhere near him.'

My response was very cagey.

Allsop's Modern-day Fables
Number 17: The Tortoise and the Hamster

Peter Jones

For Tommy Tortoise, life in twenty-first-century Britain played out as a hand-to-mouth existence full of grief and disappointment. The promise of a successful acting career varnished long ago, worn away by the grindstone of a harsh modern world. Sad old loser abandoned on benefits street, feeding off handouts and visits to the food bank, wasn't a role he ever expected to come his way.

Hard to think when Tommy made his television debut alongside Johnny Morris in Animal Magic, the media moguls talked him up as the next big thing. A series inside a Dalek on Doctor Who followed before his early success fizzled out. After that, a succession of walk-ons, voice-overs and panto kept the wolf from the door until a stroke of luck gave Tommy his big break with a part in Coronation Street.

It didn't last. His career motored downhill again when the

producers wrote Tommy's character out of the soap. Seven years playing the nation's favourite reptile, only to be squashed flat by a bin lorry while making an ill-timed dash across the cobbles. One day, propping up the long list for an Emmy, the next day, thrown onto the scrap heap. Not so much as a thank you from anybody at Granada TV.

Tommy thought his reputation would soon have people beating a path to his door with lucrative job offers. Months later, when the path lay overgrown with weeds, Tommy was forced to face the truth – the entertainment industry had moved on. Not much interest in casting an ageing, typecast thespian.

Then the virus arrived and the situation went from bad to worse. With little money coming in, Tommy maxed out his overdraft and fell behind with the rent. To top it all, the price of electricity went berserk, leaving poor Tommy with a choice between eating and heating. The tortoise shivered under a blanket all winter, cuddling a hot water bottle for company.

Not a single job offer came his way for months. Hence, a call from his agent about appearing in a commercial had Tommy dithering over the opportunity to earn a few quid. On the one hand, he needed the cash; on the other, he'd played the role a hundred times before. After some hesitation, the tortoise convinced himself a fee of a thousand pounds would pay off his credit card. The prospect of exposure on prime-time television to kick-start his career sealed the deal.

A month later, when filming day came around, Tommy arrived early on set for a final rehearsal. He went over the script until he had everything tuned to perfection; spent time practising the walk across the finish line – measured, deliberate, unhurried. A knowing wink at the camera, timed to allow some minimum-wage jobsworth to deliver the tagline: 'Amber Nectar – a taste of the slow lane'.

Tommy was in the zone, brow furrowed with concentration, going through his breathing exercises when a small voice broke the silence.

'Hiya, is this the set for the lager advert? I'm here for the Amber Nectar gig.'

That careless interruption shattered the mood. Tommy opened his eyes to find the furry head of a hamster two inches from his nose.

'Really, how rude,' Tommy snapped. 'Has no one told you never to disturb a professional while he's rehearsing? Anyway, why are you here? This is a two-hander for myself and Harry Hare. No hamster in the script. You must be in the wrong place.

'Harry's pulled a sickie,' the hamster announced. 'The agency's put me up instead.

Hammy Hamster at your service. Influencer and all-round celebrity – available for weddings and bar mitzvahs. Check out my channel on YouTube.'

Tommy rocked back with amazement, offended at the thought of working with an amateur. He couldn't stand Harry Hare, but at least the odious creature had been at RADA.

Someone would need to tell Barry Badger, the director, that the idea of subbing in an unsuitable amateur wouldn't work. Anyone with half a brain should know the tortoise and the hamster would never resonate with the great unwashed.

When Barry gathered the cast and crew together before the shoot began, Tommy barged straight in to express his worry about casting a novice for a leading part. After all, the hare role required an animal with a reputation for being zippy, and in his considered opinion, Hammy wouldn't cut it.

'I've learned a thing or two about this business over the years, let me tell you,' Tommy prattled on.

No one paid any attention to the tortoise. Barry was too busy chatting about camera angles and the like with a posse of young sidekicks.

'Hello, is anybody listening to me?' Tommy jabbed. 'I'm trying to make an important point here.'

Barry peered at the tortoise over his glasses. His upper lip curled in disdain. 'And you are?'

'Tommy Tortoise. I used to be on television, you know. Animal Magic, Dr Who, The Street and many more.'

Tommy got no further as a youthful assistant stepped in to stop him in his tracks. She confirmed the news about Harry Hare and told Barry the agency had sent a hamster to fill-in.

Much to Tommy's surprise, Barry wasn't bothered by the change of personnel. He instructed the production team to embrace the opportunity to demonstrate their adaptability. Plus, Brew Cat Brewery, who made the product, were into the equal opportunities stuff and casting had to be done blind if they were sticking to the rules.

The hamster could stay. Too late to find an alternative.

Tommy huffed and puffed, continuing to insist they must look for someone else to play Harry's part. He whittered on, explaining that the narrative was all about speed versus the subtle, sedate approach. Much to everyone's dismay, Tommy began to recite a long list of pacey creatures who could take the hare role.

His old pal, Colin, the cheetah, was first on the list. Then midway through his summary of Colin's career, Tommy remembered why the cheetah wouldn't be such an ideal candidate for the job. Not with him having recently been convicted on multiple counts of sexual assault and banged up in Strangeways prison.

The crew couldn't hide their amusement at Tommy's stuttering performance. They whispered to each other – sniggering behind their hands. Even then, Tommy couldn't let it lie. Next on his list was Walter Weasel. Walter, or his husband, Stuart Stoat, would relish the challenge.

Barry laughed, pointing out with glee that Walter and Stuart had both retired from showbiz to become bitcoin traders. Neither the stoat nor the weasel provided a realistic option, both having moved abroad to avoid paying income tax.

'No, you're stuck with Hammy, chum.' Barry sneered. 'With Brexit and all the Polish animals going back, we're already scraping the barrel with the casting for this gig.'

That sucker punch took the wind out of Tommy's sails. Even the dumb rabbit from the props department got the message. A collective burst of laughter rippled around the set.

Everyone shared the joke at Tommy's expense.

Embarrassed and beaten down, Tommy slunk off into a corner to lick his wounds. He couldn't envisage the script working with the hamster. Hammy would never convince the paying public he could outpace a tortoise. Fearing the whole thing a shambles, Tommy decided to abandon ship.

He gathered his belongings and was halfway through the door when he felt a tap on his shell. Hammy stood there, looking sheepish as anything.

Tommy gave the hamster his best withering look, perfected over many years of dealing with useless agents. He turned away with a shrug, hoping Hammy would take a hint and leave him alone.

'Give me a break, Tommy. I didn't mean to cause you a problem,' Hammy bleated. 'It's just that I need this gig, see. Standing in for Harry Hare is the first decent opportunity I've been given. The influencer stuff pays the bills but acting is my passion. It's all I've ever wanted to do. And to work alongside someone like you ... well, that would be an experience I never dreamt possible.'

The hamster had a tear in his eye. He pulled out a chequered handkerchief and blew his nose.

'I know it'll be hard, Tommy, but we can make this work if we stick together. Hear me out, coz I've got a plan.'

Tommy was torn. Lately, indecision had become his constant companion. Were it not for the necessity of financial buoyancy, he'd call it a draw right now. What to do?

Back in the day, Tommy would've thrown a strop and walked away, confident in the knowledge the director would rush after him, begging him to return. Kicked off big time, demanding that he got his way. But now he was too tired to argue. Tommy hadn't the energy for a fight, so he nodded for the hamster to continue.

Seeing his opportunity, Hammy sprang into action, keen to

explain how the two of them might play the scene to best effect.

'You're gonna love this, Tom,' he began. 'The secret is how we frame our characters from the off. When we get to the starting line, I'll look like I'm raring to go. You do your famous can't-be-arsed, nonchalant act. Munch some green stuff or something. Give it the old vacant stare. Three, two, one, bang, and I'm away. Legging it like Usain Bolt.'

Once he got to the allotments, Hammy planned to dodge into the hedge and hide out there for half an hour. Meanwhile, Tommy could toddle along at a relaxed pace until he reached the post box, where an Uber would be waiting.

'Uber?' All too much for Tommy. By now, the poor tortoise was totally confused.

Hammy explained how he'd booked Tommy an Uber on his mobile to save the tortoise's legs – paid for from Barry's budget.

Hammy had everything figured out. The Uber would drop Tommy off at the top of the hill before the finish, where the hamster's sister, Hetty, would meet him. She'd spray the tortoise with water to make it look as if he'd come the whole distance under his own steam. Then, Hetty would rub some grease on the bottom of Tommy's shell, give him a push and away he'd go. Just like on Ski Sunday.

The whole thing sounded ridiculous to Tommy. However, considering his status in the acting profession, a taxi ride was the least the studio could do to make amends for his shabby treatment. He decided to play along.

'Don't worry. It'll be easy,' the hamster promised. 'Can't go wrong, trust me. Oh, and one more thing, before we set off, can I please have your autograph? My mum loved you in Corrie.'

When the cameras rolled, the two animals played their respective parts like consummate

professionals. Tommy couldn't help feeling a twinge of guilt at how he doubted Hammy. The animal certainly could act – truly the Leonardo DiCaprio of rodents.

Three, two, one, bang. Off went Hammy, racing up the hill and disappearing around the corner. Tommy nibbled away at a lettuce leaf, laying on the Mr Nonchalant shtick with all the skill of an old hand. Then he ambled up the road.

Tommy waited at the post box, but there was no Uber. Without a taxi ride to speed him on his journey, he struggled along, slowly placing one tired leg in front of the other. Mile after mile until hours later, he reached the finish line and collapsed in a heap. Exhausted from his efforts, Tommy consoled himself with the thought of the cheque, which would soon be nestling in his bank account.

'Where've you been?' demanded Barry Badger. 'We were just about to send out a search party. Hammy's been and gone ages ago. Lucky for you, I've got all the shots I need. I can still make the footage work with a spot of clever editing on my laptop.'

Tommy couldn't believe it. He'd tried his best but had been let down by the taxi. When he mentioned the problem with the Uber by way of an excuse, Barry stared at him as if he were mad.

'Uber? What Uber?' Barry yelled. 'We haven't got the money for an Uber. Next you'll want different coloured lettuce leaves in your dressing room.'

Leaving Tommy flat out on the grass verge, the badger and his assistant began to pack up the remains of their kit. As the final piece went in the van, Barry turned to the tortoise.

'Anyway, a generous gesture, Tommy, giving your fee to charity.'

A look of despair spread over the tortoise's face. He hadn't a clue what the badger was talking about. Other than a few payments back in the day to the Tommy Tortoise Retirement Fund, he'd always made it a principle never to give anything to charity.

'Come on.' Barry sniggered. 'Hammy said you two were doing the gig for Young Animals in Need. He gave me the form with details of your Just Giving page, and I transferred the money like you wanted. Don't play the innocent, Tommy. You signed the thing.'

A very stressed tortoise stared back, looking totally bemused. The story of a charitable donation was news to him.

Suddenly, Barry burst out laughing.

'Bloody hell, I get it now. That hamster has pulled a fast one. You've been had, fella. Ha, ha.'

Barry threw his head back, holding his sides, unable to hide his amusement at how easily Tommy had fallen for the scam played on him by Hammy. Still gagging with laughter, the badger jumped in his van and roared off down the road, desperate to tell the lads at the Chicken and Anthropologist how the famous Tommy Tortoise had been done over by a hamster.

Tommy lay there, alone, his mind in a daze. After a while, he picked himself up and wandered off to find the bus back home.

'Country's going to the dogs,' he muttered as he limped down the street. 'Larry Fox has it right. No one is safe anymore. Bring back hanging, I say. Send all the immigrants to Rwanda. That'll stop the rot, except the place is full of woke lefties, and nothing will be done.'

Moral: Te dormis, te perdere. In today's cut-throat world, winning is the business of life.

Anybody daft enough to think a hamster can operate a mobile phone to call a taxi is fair game.

P.S. It wouldn't have mattered anyway, because it's common knowledge – Uber won't carry animals. Doh!

The Hamster's Got Laser Eyes

Gina Devine

Suzy got to the bottom of the stairs, rubbing the sleep from her eyes. The curtains hadn't been opened yet, but the sun was shining in through the gaps. She could hear Mum and Dad arguing quietly in the kitchen. That meant they were trying to keep their voices down, but it was getting louder.

'Morning,' she called out, to let them know she was here.

It went quiet in the kitchen for a moment, followed by frantic loud whispering. Suzy crept a little closer to hear what was being said.

'It doesn't look anything like her other hamster,' her mum said.

'It's the same sort of colour and about the same size,' her dad replied.

'She'll know. And where did you get it from anyway? The pet shop won't be open at this time.'

'That guy from work. You know – can get hold of anything,

he said he needed to get rid of this one quickly because--'

'Shhh!'

There was a sneeze from the other end of the living room; it was Robby playing on his phone.

'Morning, Robby,' Suzy said to her brother. Robby grunted but didn't say anything.

'Good morning, everyone, what a cheerful day it is,' she said, dripping with sarcasm. The kitchen door opened and her mum and dad shuffled out of the kitchen awkwardly.

Dad clearly had something behind his back.

'I'm sorry, darling,' Mum said, 'but your hamster got out in the night. We only spotted this morning and have been looking everywhere for him. Thankfully, your dad managed to get him back from under the sofa. Isn't that good news?'

'Here you go, Suzy, safe and sound,' Dad said holding out a tiny cage with a hamster in it.

It was very similar, the same sort of colouring, same size, but it moved differently. The way it twitched its nose looked different too.

'Where did you get the little case from?' Suzy asked.

'Oh, er, this old thing?' Dad said, eyes twitching side to side. 'It was in the garage. We got it ages ago, when we first got the hamster.'

'Yeah, that was it,' Mum said unconvincingly.

Suzy frowned at them both, then walked over to pick up the little cage and see who was inside.

'There you go,' Dad said as he handed it over. 'Mr Fluffykins is back safe and sound.'

Mum rolled her eyes. She never liked the name, it was one

Dad had suggested. And whilst it wasn't what she's ideally wanted to call a pet, it did at least seem to annoy Robby, so she'd stuck with Mr Fluffykins.

Suzy took the mini cage over to the hamster cage at the other end of the living room, walking past Robby to get there. She peered into the cage and the hamster peered back at her. She couldn't be sure, but the hamster seemed much more inquisitive. Mr Fluffykins – the real one – just tended to stare into empty space most of the time. It moved about, ate food, slept and left tiny hamster poo everywhere, but other than that it seemed a bit too relaxed. This one on the other hand looked positively shrewd by comparison. She peered more closely at it and the hamster glanced sideways then stared back at her and shrugged, as if to say, 'What?'

'This hamster's weird,' she said quietly.

'You're weird,' Robby replied.

'And you're still dumber than this hamster,' she said, expecting Robby's reply. 'I'm serious. Look at it.'

She held the cage close to Robby's head.

'Get that thing away from me,' he said and flicked the bars with a finger, making a small clanking sound.'

'Don't do that you idiot!' she yelled.

She pulled the cage away carefully and set it down next to the big hamster cage on the side. This may not be her hamster, but it didn't deserve to be treated like that.

'Sorry little dude,' she said as she opened the hatch on the side. The hamster was staring out of the cage at Robby; it looked annoyed. 'Come on, let's get you inside shall we?'

Suzy brought the little cage over and then opened the door

to the little cage so that it could climb across. But the hamster turned and stared at her.

'Well go on then, this is where you live ... now.'

The hamster appeared to roll its eyes before stepping cautiously into the big cage. It hopped in, picked up bits of sawdust with its tiny front paws, sniffed them, then dropped them again. It scampered around the hamster cage, investigating every level, peering behind every corner and leaving no space unvisited. Bits of sawdust and bedding had been flung through the gaps in the fine metal bars. Suzy started to collect bits off the carpet when Robby leaned over and started banging his phone on the top of the cage.

'Welcome home, stinky.'

Robby laughed as the hamster darted about wildly.

'Robby, you shit!'

'Suzy!' Mum shouted, 'we don't use language like that!'

'But Robby's being mean to the––'

There was a flash and a popping sound.

'My phone!' Robby cried.

His mobile phone was cracked and smoking, as Robbie turned it over Suzy could see a small hole in the back with blackened scorch marks around it. He prodded at the screen and the side buttons, but it clearly wasn't working anymore.

'Your stupid hamster did that!' Robbie moaned. 'It ... did something weird.'

'Don't be thick, it's a hamster. You must have done it.'

'How?' Robby held up the smoking device.

It did seem unusual that Robby could, or even would, damage his own phone like that. But what else could it have been? It obviously couldn't have been the hamster. Could it?

Dad's phone rang and he answered.

'Hello?' he said. 'Oh hello, yes, yes, OK yes, oh dear, is she all right?'

'Who is it?' Mum asked.

'It's Gran, she's had a fall,' Dad whispered across. 'Yes, OK, so shall I … oh dear, that badly? OK. Well I'm sure we can both come. Yes, we'll be there in … thirty minutes?' Mum nodded to Dad 'OK, we'll see you then.'

'What's wrong?' Suzy asked.

'So, you probably heard, Gran's had a fall,' Dad replied. 'Sounds like it might be quite bad. Mum and I are going to drive over there now, can you two please get on with each other while we're out, OK? It's an hour there and back, plus however long it takes to look after Gran.'

'Whatever,' Robby said as he stomped off upstairs.

Mum and Dad grabbed their shoes and coats and left quickly. She heard the car drive away, and then just like that, the house seemed empty.

'Just you and me then, Mr Fluffykins, or whoever you are.'

Before she had time to think about it any further, there was a knock at the door. Suzy peered out of the window; there was no car or van there for a delivery.

'Hello there, young lady, is your mum or dad in?' A youngish woman in a very smart-looking brown suit said. She was holding a clipboard and had lanyard and ID card around her neck. Nothing Suzy recognised though.

'No sorry, they've just gone out,' Suzy replied. 'Who should I say called?'

'Oh dear, do you know when they're due back?'

Suzy thought for a moment. This person seemed fairly official but she didn't want to tell her there wouldn't be any adults in the house for quite a while.

'Not sure. They could be back any minute.'

'Oh, OK.' The woman seemed surprised by Suzy's answer for a moment, but then gave a frown as she answered: 'You see, I work for the council and really need to speak to the owner of the house about the boundaries at the front.'

'Don't you have all that stuff at the council?'

'Ha ha, I can see you're a bright girl aren't you? I bet you don't need adults tell you what's what all the time?'

That seemed an odd thing to say. 'What d'you mean?'

'Oh, it's nothing. I just find that adults often underestimate smart children like yourself. For instance, I bet you're bright enough to show me where the front boundary of your house is.'

Suzy thought about it for a minute. She had a pretty good idea of where the boundary was, it wasn't difficult tell. It just seemed a really odd thing for someone from the council wanting to get a child to confirm.

'I'm twelve. I'm not taking responsibility for that. You can speak to my mum and dad when they're back.'

'Yes, probably a good idea.' The woman said pleasantly. 'Would it be all right if I come in and wait for them?'

'No, of course not!'

The woman was glancing over Suzy's shoulder, towards the kitchen and shaking her head.

'What are you doing?'

Suzy glanced behind and spotted a muscly but rather dopey-looking man creeping in through the back door and into the kitchen. He was wearing a green tracksuit with white trainers and a white baseball cap.

'Hey, who are you? Get out!'

'Oh very subtle.' The woman at the door said to the man, who stopped creeping and just shrugged. 'You were supposed to wait until she was out of sight? Oh never mind.'

She gave a big sigh and then shoved Suzy backwards into the house, stepped inside and shut the door behind her.

'Right young lady, go and get your mum and dad's jewellery, any laptops, tablets, games consoles. You know, anything of value.'

'What? Why would I––'

'Well, either you help us get what we need, or we tie you up, gag you and stick you in a cupboard somewhere out of the way.'

'What?'

Suit-woman shrugged and looked at the tracksuit guy. 'Fetch the tie tags and Duck Tape®.'

'Did you bring that or was I supposed to, erm, you know?' tracksuit-guy stammered.

'In the bag, the bag you were supposed to bring from the car?'

Tracksuit-guy gave a thumbs up, removed his backpack and started rummaging through the contents.

'Today would be good. Honestly!'

Tracksuit-guy pulled out a baseball bat, followed by a big roll of thick black tape and some very large and solid-looking tie tags. Suzy saw both of them were distracted briefly and made a run for the stairs, but suit-woman grabbed her arm and dragged her back again.

'Not so fast, young lady,' she said through clenched teeth, before turning to tracksuit-guy. 'Can you please incapacitate her?'

Tracksuit-guy picked up the baseball bat.

'With the tape and tie tags!'

Tracksuit-guy shrugged, put down the bat and began to restrain Suzy with the tie tags.

'Dad knows Karate and Mum's lethal with the kitchen knives, you know,' Suzy said.

'And I'm a black belt in origami.' Suit-woman replied. 'Shut her up will you. With the tape!'

Tracksuit-guy tied Suzy up. She wriggled and squealed but couldn't get free.

'Erm. Oh, stick her in that corner, near the guinea pig, or whatever it is. We'll get the big screen on the way out. Check upstairs for jewellery and stuff first.'

Tracksuit-guy placed Suzy carefully on the floor, but not before she got a swift, two- footed kick to the guy's knee that almost knocked him over.

Suit-woman glared at her.

'Try that again and I'll let him use the bat.'

Suzy decided to wait quietly until the pair disappeared upstairs, but then she realised Robby was up there. Would he do something stupid? Of course he would, he's Robby. She waited a bit longer, still no sound. Something wasn't right. Perhaps he was hiding, that would be a sensible thing to do.

Ugh! She needed to get free.

She wriggled around, looking for something to cut the ties with, like they did in the movies. It was only now that she appreciated how unhelpful 'family friendly' furniture was when you needed to escape from restraints. She really hated the tape across her mouth, but thankfully tracksuit-guy hadn't done a very good job and she was able to rub her mouth across her shoulder to pull it free.

New Mr Fluffykins, or Mr Fluffykins mk2, was peering through the bars quite intently at what was going on.

'Don't suppose you can get me free can you?' Suzy asked with a chuckle. 'You know, chew through these ties or something?'

The hamster didn't make a sound but appeared to shrug its shoulders.

'Well, if you do have laser eyes, or whatever you used on Robby's phone, it would be really handy to get out of these cable ties.'

No sooner had she spoken than tiny orange lasers shot from the hamster's eyes, cutting the ties and releasing her in an instant.

'What the heck! I was only joking. I didn't think … oh wow!'

Suzy pulled the tape off the side of her face and removed the remains of the cable ties. There was a loud crash and several thuds, followed by some shouting. Clearly the burglars had found Robby, or Robby had found them. There were some more noises shortly before tracksuit-guy and suit-woman came down the stairs carrying Robby, all tied up and taped.

'Right you can lie there in the corner with your--' Suit-woman stared wide-eyed at Suzy. 'How the hell did you get out? Some kind of Houdini trick?' She jabbed tracksuit-guy in the arm. 'Stick that one in the corner and tie her up again. Properly this time!'

Tracksuit-guy sighed, then lugged Robby over to the corner of the room. Suzy stood to the side of the hamster cage, making sure the path was clear.

'I don't think so,' Suzy said with a smug grin. 'Mr Fluffykins, perhaps you could free Robby too?'

Nothing happened. Suzy looked down at the cage to see Mr Fluffykins staring back at her.

'Oh come on, he only tapped your cage. These are actual bad guys!'

The hamster shook its head and then lasered Robby free. Robby scrambled to his feet looking bewildered, probably not sure who to be more afraid of.

'That mouse,' said tracksuit-guy, 'it just ... you know, with its eyes!'

'It's a hamster,' Suzy corrected him, 'and his name is Mr Fluffykins, bitch!'

'Shut her up,' suit-woman said calmly, 'then we grab the expensive goods and we leave. OK? Surely it's not that difficult for a body builder, like you, to handle a couple of kids and a hamster?'

'But the eyes,' he replied, pleading.

'Just hit the rodent with the baseball bat!'

Tracksuit-guy shook his head, gave an apologetic shrug, picked up the bat and made his way toward the hamster cage.

'Get them, Mr Fluffykins! Destroy them!' Suzy roared

maniacally.

The hamster's eyes began to glow orange, getting brighter and brighter, before it unleashed a barrage of lasers, firing down relentlessly upon the two hapless intruders. First the baseball bat was cut to splinters, next tracksuit-guy was zapped head to toe, singeing his hair, burning holes in his tracksuit and destroying his trainers. Suit-woman, who had thrown her clipboard at the hamster cage and grabbed a knife from the rucksack, had been showered with splinters of clipboard, the knife zapped until the blade fell off. Her hair was singed, her suit ruined and heeled shoes all but destroyed.

The two intruders had no choice but to run screaming from the house, grabbing what was left of their belonging on the way out.

No sooner had they left when Mum and Dad walked in.

'What on earth happened here?' Mum asked.

'Mum! Dad! You're home already,' Suzy said with relief.

'Yes, Mum called Gran's care home on the way to see if she needed anything,' Dad said. 'They said no one had called us and that Gran was fine, so we were worried something was going on.'

'I think it's OK now,' Suzy said with a smile. 'And thank you for finding Mr Fluffykins, Dad.'

'Definitely!' said Robby.

Not Everyone Comes Out Smelling of Roses

Karen Ette

'You're late!'

Paige took a deep breath and turned to face the bar manager, who glared at her through bottle-bottom specs, cheeks reddening and his piggy eyes narrowing to almost a slit.

'Mr Bloodwort, I am not late. Queen Victoria is late, Winston Churchill is late, I am very much alive and therefore not late, unlike Jonas Henson who until yesterday was not late, in fact, he was here, sitting in your bar drinking Timothy Taylor's until closing. Sadly, he is now the late Jonas Henson.' Paige shrugged her coat off and stuffed it under the bar. She turned around and began to check the optics.

'What do you mean he's late?'

'Oh for goodness' sake, you're the landlord of the village pub, the font of all gossip, and you didn't even know that he was found down by the railway line?'

Liam Bloodwort was frowning. Paige watched him open and close his mouth like a goldfish on its continuous cycle of discovery in a spherical tank.

'Is he … is he all right?'

How stupid is this man, Paige thought.

'No of course he isn't all right. I've just told you – he's dead.'

'Did he …??'

'Did he what?'

'You know …' Liam Bloodwort cocked his head to one side in question.

'I don't know. Apparently he had sustained serious injuries; no doubt we shall soon find out. Isn't it time you unlocked the doors? It's past opening – and you're late.' Paige couldn't help herself and she smiled as she watched him draw back the heavy bolts on the front doors.

*

'I'll have another Islay please.' Wesley leant against the bar and handed his glass over.

'Any more news on Jonas Henson?' Paige asked as she took the glass.

'No, but I have found out that the remains of someone called Anthony Reed was found beside the railway track twenty years ago. It's a cold case and was assumed suicide but never proven. Apparently, he'd died at least ten years before he was found but wild boar and decomposition had pretty well destroyed any evidence.'

'We could do with DI Sandbach to help solve that mystery.'

'He's on annual leave and holidaying beside the seaside.'

'Sandbach at the seaside? Whatever next.'

'Do you think the two deaths are connected?'

'No idea – until we know if this is a suicide we've nothing to go on.' Wesley took the glass of peaty amber liquid that Paige was passing to him.

A young man with what Paige called a 'happy face' came to the bar and placed two empty glasses down.

'Same again, please.'

'Timothy Taylors?' Paige lifted both glasses and smiled.

'Please. Haven't seen you in here before, you new?'

'I started last week, I'm Paige,' she said as the first pint glass filled. 'And you are?'

'Joe, Joseph Kwanena.'

'What a lovely name, I haven't heard that before.'

'It's because I was born on a Saturday. They call me Kawme at the surgery.'

'Surgery?' Paige handed Joe his pint.

'Yes, Ivy House, I'm a vet. That's Pete Johnson over there.'

Joe indicated to the man sitting by the fire still wearing his green fleece with a gold ivy emblem on the sleeve. 'He's more farm and horses, I prefer smaller animals.'

Paige handed over the second pint and pushed the card reader towards Joe.

'Ooh, what have you done to your hand? It can't be easy treating animals with a bandage around it.'

Joe looked down and laughed. He took his card and said:

'Hamster bit me.'

'Oh dear, how come?'

'A young lad brought it in yesterday. It had an abscess so I said I would give it an antibiotic injection. The little boy looked terrified so I told him to go and sit in the waiting room. I picked the hamster up and it sunk its teeth into my hand.'

'Did the injection work?'

'I didn't get that far, I pulled my hand away backwards but it was still attached and I accidentally flung it at the wall.'

'Is it all right?'

'Not exactly, the impact killed it. I had to tell the little lad that it didn't survive the injection.' Joe picked up the two pints of Timothy Taylors, winked at Paige and turned to join his fellow vet.

'Are you blushing?' Wesley asked.

'No, but he is very charming.'

'Hm, I wouldn't trust him, just watch out.'

'Are you jealous?' Paige teased.

'No, of course not.'

'Yes you are, and I'm sure he's trustworthy.'

'How can you trust a man who kills hamsters?'

'It was an accident.'

'Any breakages, accidental or otherwise, will be deducted from your wages,' Liam Bloodwort came into the bar from his office.

Oh great, thought Paige, he's here again, listening.

'I haven't broken anything, Mr Bloodwort, don't worry.'

The manager walked away again, tutting.

'I don't think he likes you,' Wesley said.

'Well, I don't like him, and he smells. How much longer do I need to be here? Can't we go somewhere nice like a pacific island rather than here in February?'

'Patience, sweetheart. I just need to pop back thirty years and I've found the perfect gate to go through to take me there.'

'Don't forget to come back for me, or at least tell me where the gate is.'

'It's just behind the church, but I'll be back.'

Paige pulled her coat tighter as she walked towards the pub and her next morning shift. A police car passed her, then another, lights on but no sirens.

She went through the usual routine of checking optics, mixers, crisps, nuts and was thankful she didn't have to clean ashtrays as she had when she had done similar work in the 1970s.

The shift dragged with few casual callers, no doubt it would liven up in the evening. She glanced at the clock over the bell that would signal 'time'. Just one more hour and she could head home.

A couple who had been in for coffee called goodbye and headed towards the door and as they left two police officers entered. Their radios crackled. Paige smiled.

'Good morning, miss, is the manager in? We'd like to ask a few questions.'

'Of course. Mr Bloodwort, two police officers to see you,' Paige called.

Liam Bloodwort came into the bar and said to Paige: 'You

125

can go now, your shift's almost over.'

'We'd prefer it if you stayed, miss,' one of the officers said.

'Come through to my office.' Liam Bloodwort seemed insistent.

'We're fine here, thank you.'

Paige said nothing and waited for whatever questions they might have.

'Has anyone from the Ivy House veterinary surgery been in lately?'

'Yes, two came--'

'I'll handle this,' Liam Bloodwort said. 'I believe we have had them as customers recently.'

What an arse, thought Paige.

'And who were they, sir?'

'Erm, well, I don't know, I didn't ask them their names, I just saw them in here the other night.'

'It was Joseph Kwanena and Pete Johnson. Are they in trouble?'

'Mr Johnson seems to have gone missing, he hasn't been to work, his house is empty but his car is still there, as is his mobile phone. His last call-out was at the farm on Big Lane that's set back from the road about half-a-mile. He didn't turn up to the next one at the stables.'

'The pig farm?' Paige asked. 'Sorry, I haven't seen either of them since the other night.'

'Thank you, miss, sir. Have a good day.'

The officers left and Liam Bloodwort shot the bolts across.

'I'm closing for the afternoon, be back at six,' he told Paige.

Thankful for the early closure, Paige hurried home where

Wesley had returned. She hugged him and told him about Pete Johnson's disappearance.

'I think we need to visit the farm,' Wesley said. 'I have found some information but if this is connected then it's not making sense – yet.'

Paige pulled her scarf over her nose, the smell was making her eyes water.

'Ow do,' a man in a filthy green boiler suit called over to them. Paige concentrated on keeping her footing – she didn't want to slip over in the quagmire.

'Good afternoon, sir,' Wesley said, but didn't offer to shake the man's hand. 'We're from the Pig Wellness and Safety Board, just paying a routine visit, won't take a moment. May we see the pigs please?'

'They're over there.'

'Thank you, won't be long,' Wesley said and walked in the direction the farmer had indicated. Paige followed. The smell was even worse inside the pens.

'The Pig Wellness and Safety Board? What the hell's that?' Paige asked.

'No idea, but it worked didn't it?'

'What are you looking for?'

'I'm not sure.'

'Then what on earth are we doing here?'

Wesley didn't answer; he walked along the pens to the farrowing crates where sows lay on their sides in the filth and piglets squealed as they took as much from their mothers as they could.

Paige stopped just before the crates and reached over the gate of the end pen.

'Everything all right?' The gruff voice was coming from the open doorway. Paige quickly pushed her hand into her coat pocket and spun around.

'There might be a problem with one of your gilts.' Wesley had come back from the farrowing crates and was looking into a pen of young sows.

'I will need to return with a vet before I can give you the wellness and safety certificate.'

'Never 'ad one afore,' the farmer said and spat on the floor. 'Don't want no veterinary here; they cost too much.'

'They'll be paid for by the Board, Mr?'

The farmer turned his back and began walking away. 'No choice then, have I?' he called over his shoulder. 'But keep out of the farrowing crates, don't want you upsetting the sows, they can be nasty, tha' knows.'

'Thank you, Mr? We'll be back shortly.'

The church clock struck three.

'I really should change before I go back to work,' Paige said, sniffing her hair, 'or I'll smell like Liam Bloodwort.'

Paige pushed her hand into her pocket, pulled out a scrap of material and handed it to Wesley.

'Where did you find this?' he asked.

'It was caught on a nail by the last pig pen. Can you see what it is?'

'It's green fleece.'

'Yes, the same green as the vets have, and look.' She

pointed to the frayed edge. 'That looks like a piece of the gold ivy leaf.'

'We need to go back to the farm with the other vet, Kwame did you say?'

'Why, what's he done?'

'Nothing, but I told the farmer that we'd be back with the vet to examine the pigs.'

'Are you going to tell me what's going on?'

'I'll tell you on the way. Where's Sandbach when you need him?'

'You told me, he's at the seaside!'

'Then those two plods will have to do.' He indicated at the police car that was parked by the farm gate. 'Run and get Joseph Kwanena and bring him to the farm, just tell him he needs to check out one of the gilts.'

Wesley was deep in conversation with the farmer when Paige and the vet arrived.

'Ah, here's the vet now.' Wesley raised his voice, 'Thank you, Mr Smith, we'll head over to the pens. We'll try not to hold you up for too long.'

'I never told you my name,' growled the farmer.

'So you didn't,' Wesley said, and smiled. He nodded towards the police car and then walked over to the pig pens. Paige and Joseph followed him.

'Which gilt is unwell?' Joseph asked.

'None of them,' said Wesley, 'but I needed you here to authenticate our presence otherwise he wouldn't have let us in.

'I'll wait here,' Paige said, the smell was too overpowering.

Wesley and Joseph walked past the farrowing crates and into the grain store far end of the building.

'Ah, I thought I'd find you here,' Wesley said.

Liam Bloodwort spun around. 'You! What do you want?'

'I want you to open the trapdoor that you have just closed.'

Liam Bloodwort ran from the store towards the yard. Joseph moved to go after him but Wesley said: 'Leave him, you need to get your colleague out of the cellar.'

Paige was watching the two police officers talking with the farmer when Liam Bloodwort rushed from the pig pens. He barged past her but not before she could give him a hefty shove. He stumbled, tried to regain his balance but slipped and fell into the slurry pit.

Wesley came out followed by Joseph and a semi-conscious Pete Johnson. Joseph looked horrified when he saw Liam Bloodwort floundering in the slurry.

'We have to get him out,' he shouted, 'or he'll drown in there.'

'No he won't,' said Paige, 'it's only waist-high, we'll leave him for the boys in blue.'

More police arrived and an ambulance for Pete Johnson, who had obviously been beaten and drugged. While the paramedics tended to Pete, Joseph walked over to Paige and Wesley.

'How did you know? And what's all this got to do with Pete?'

'It's complicated, but once I could unravel it all, it made sense. You see the farmer, over there?' Wesley pointed across the yard. 'Well, his father was a prisoner of war in 1945,

Dereq Schmidt. He marries a farmer's daughter and only child called Jane Brown. She inherits the farm when her father dies and they have a son, Derek – that's him talking to the police.

Dereq Schmidt, however, was a bit of a lad and had a fling with a neighbour called Sally Reed; they had a son, Anthony, who marries Lily Bloodwort. Anthony and Lily have four children, including Liam Bloodwort, the youngest. When Dereq Schmidt dies, he leaves the farm to our friendly farmer, Derek. Anthony wants half the farm as they are half-brothers. In an argument, Derek kills Anthony and buries him in farmland where he wasn't discovered for ten years.'

'But where does Pete fit in? Why was he in the cellar?' Joseph asked.

'Wrong place at the wrong time, unfortunately for him.'

Pete looked up from the stretcher he had been placed on. 'I overheard an argument between Smith and Bloodwort; Bloodwort said he wanted half of what the farm was worth otherwise he would tell the police that Smith killed Anthony Reed and Jonas Henson.'

'Jonas Henson!' Paige said.

'Yes, he's Lily and Anthony's grandson and was trying to get the case into Anthony's death reopened.'

'So Bloodwort knew damn well that it wasn't suicide.'

'Indeed he did.'

'What will happen to the farm now?' Joseph asked.

'That's for the lawyers to decide,' Wesley said. 'Not our problem.'

They watched the blue lights from the ambulance and police cars disappearing down the lane.

'I don't envy the ones who have a stinking Bloodwort with them,' said Paige. 'It's getting dark and I need to get home for a shower,'

'I think we both need a shower,' Wesley said and winked at her.

'Come on you, let's get back, it's almost opening time.'

Between a Rock and a Soft Place

Alix Ashurst

The rebellion was not progressing as planned.

As the raging sun cast strident prison-bar shadows across the urine-stained sawdust, General Fluffkins contemplated just how much longer she would have to endure this humiliating torment. Contained in a nauseatingly cheerful turquoise tray, by four airy, yet still strangely oppressive, caged walls, she felt 'in limbo', waiting wearily, day after day, night after night … for goodness only knows what.

This is not how things were supposed to go down. In an increasingly distant memory, she painfully recalled how her mother had pushed her away, along with all her siblings – no bad thing, to be fair, as the boys particularly had begun to get a bit frisky. But the truth was real – for no fathomable reason, she just wasn't welcome in the soft, warm embraces of a loving parent. She'd been forcibly cast out, naked into the world and expected to make it on her own.

She'd stayed with her sister for a while at the muster-station. It was an inconsequential dorm, with a hard, clear surface completely across one side of it, beyond which lurched a great, grey chasm stretching out far beyond sight. The floor was casually strewn with wood chips, dry seeds and hard pellets. A large, drippy nozzle poked down from above to provide liquid sustenance. And one corner had a shredded, papery mass that was presumably supposed to serve as a bed. All too frequently, impossibly huge, hairless faces would materialise out of the blurry distance beyond the chasm, casting great shadows, grotesquely giggling too loudly and banging on the invisible wall. For the rest of the day, peculiar, detached commotions would echo around, chattering and beeping and disturbing her already all too brief sleep.

But at least the nights were less busy, and then there were happier moments too.

Sometimes she could hear her brothers laughing and joking between alcoves nearby. Though she couldn't see them, she knew their unforgettable voices and would sometimes join in with their banter. Other times, she just liked to listen and remember how cosy it was when they were all simply snuggled up together ... with their mother close by. Bliss.

There were other voices she could hear too: a lolloping, twitchy, friendly fellow from somewhere in the mists below; a squeaky, snuffly sort over to the left; a softly spoken, silky lass who seemed to take sincere pleasure in persistently shushing everyone; a fast-talking insurgent known simply as Pepper and a gaggle of shy, squeaky ladies who just chipped in occasionally with words of harmonious approval or assembled disgust.

Her favourite by far, however, was the squawky, old, flappy chap who loved to regale them with tales of his former life. He described places you could scarcely dream of: forests of broad green leaves that grew abundantly on immeasurably tall trees; vast mountains with rocky walls reaching high into the clouds; great expanses of water that caressed sun-drenched shores and golden beaches; immense, wide deserts filled with hot sands and skittish creatures; savannahs, plains, waterfalls. Words you could barely make sense of but that sounded so intoxicatingly exotic.

What tremendous wonders there must be beyond the great chasm! she thought, night after night, as she casually gnawed away on unexpectedly tasty crispy flakes and wheaty pellets.

She longed to go adventuring and exploring. What smells? What delights? Everything 'out there' just sounded so entirely marvellous. Squawky could transport their imaginations all night long with his enchanting descriptions.

Pepper, however, had a different take on things. She had a down for every up and somehow managed to steer every conversation round to the 'Righteous Revolution' that she was determined to bring about – how could the world be 'entirely marvellous' when evil, skulking creatures were still out there?

She was clearly a social creature, but something was glaringly absent – something, or maybe, someone – a yin for her yang. Occasionally, there was a half-spoken word, a name, perhaps, that of a long-lost companion, caught and then rapidly trampled in the pace of her words. Or there'd be a wistful air in her tone that betrayed a sense grief – a profound and enduring sadness that despite leaving her unsettled was also, unmistakably, the very fuel in her fire. Nothing short of acute revenge could penetrate, or even begin to sooth, her resentment.

She confidently rallied them all to her way of thinking and then began forming a plan.

General Fluffkins, thankfully, had never known the evil that Pepper spoke of, but of course, she understood loss and pain and so she deeply wanted to do anything she could to help her miserable comrade. Justice would be served so that joy could follow – after all, wasn't that every creature's fair and natural right? So, along with everyone else, she busied herself in preparation. Pepper said the first step was 'observation'. 'Take note of everything!' she commanded. 'Opportunities, timings, changes – anything we can exploit to our advantage. We can't do anything whilst we're trapped in here – we must escape!'

As part of her observations, General Fluffkins realised that there was always a moment when their food arrived – it had to come in from somewhere. Sometimes when the faces appeared, she suspected the clear wall would move magically over to one side – although she never knew this for certain as, well, for one thing, it would usually happen when they were fast asleep during the day. And for another, on the occasions when they were awake, it was such a terrifying disruption that they would instinctively run and hide in the relative safety of their bedding. Nevertheless, she knew there had to be a way for the food to get in ... and wherever it was ... that could be their way out ... if only they could pluck up the courage to stand fast and see. Maybe they could wedge something in the gap to keep it open, a seed perhaps, or maybe a pellet?

Regrettably, as time passed, slowly, steadily, one by one, the familiar voices disappeared, replaced only by strangers who knew nothing of their long-endured trials. Frighteningly, it wasn't long before she woke one morning to find her sister gone too. She recollected how she'd franticly searched their sparse apartment, but of course, to no avail. A deep, half-remembered emptiness swamped her troubled reminiscing and her thoughts returned willingly to her present reality – her strangely cosy turquoise corner cobbled together out of discarded papers – her small oasis in the ultimate abyss that seemed to stretch far beyond her now lonely life.

When she too had finally been removed from the muster-station, she'd been squashed into an incredibly claustrophobic box and shaken around, perhaps even gleefully, until she was discourteously slid out into this new, soon-to-be all-too-familiar, turquoise penitentiary. The resounding, clanking latch coldly clamping shut her brief, but boldly ambitious, plans of getting the gang back together – of breaking free and adventuring out into the great wide world that Squawky had longingly described. Pepper's insistent words that once rang in her ears – 'They must pay' – now, silenced ... lost ... gone forever ... forgotten. No, maybe not forgotten, never forgotten, just parked, resting, or perhaps ... just recharging? The rebellion would rise again – 'as long as we have breath in our bodies!'

Yet, who was she now? A shadow of her former self, she'd lost her drive – her ambition was clearly too busy taking a nap to answer back. She snuggled deeper into her soft warm bedding. Maybe, she could just steal a few more moments of temporary comfort before getting back into some serious training. After all, whatever was going to happen, it would always be important to be fit and ready for action at a moment's notice. Pepper couldn't say it enough – 'Stay fit! Stay fearless!'

Occasionally, the roof of her home would be raised to the sky and fleshy grabbers would close securely around her, scooping her up high into the air and then setting her down, albeit ever-so-gently. When it had first happened, of course, she'd been completely terrified but to her great delight, she'd soon found that this was by far the best training ground. There would be climbing walls to negotiate, tunnels to explore, moving walkways overlapping, turning this way and that, and occasionally even a soft, warm rest spot so she could catch her breath. Sometimes, she also liked to spread herself out flat on a cold, hard surface to cool down, and from here she could sneakily observe. No bars, no chasms, no clear walls in her way, she could easily just scamper off at any time. But she didn't – not yet anyway. She couldn't deny she loved it all! So much fun! Even though the big faces would be there again too, now they had kinder voices, uncluttered by the muster-station's layers of cacophonous noises and beeps. They simply sounded happy and amused.

Eventually, however, she would still be returned to her tight turquoise box. Though each time it would smell sweeter again with fresh supplies of bedding materials, food and clean water. Frustrating as it was to have to keep tearing up and remaking her cosy sleeping chamber, she began to appreciate the crisp, clean newness it also brought. Each evening as she woke ready to take on the world, she began to think twice about climbing out of her perfectly round nest and often snuzzled down for a few moments more bliss. What was it she had planned to do? There had been something important, something pressing. Something to observe ... something she'd been wanting to do, waiting to do. Clearly, she was still waiting. So perhaps she could wait a while longer - for now anyway.

Meeeeooowwww! What on earth was that? Her world shifted sideways as an excruciating sound pierced the air. Her bedding slid violently across the floor, though fortuitously keeping her safely cocooned inside. Poom! Poom! Again, she felt the planet shake. Tentatively, she twitched her whiskers – what was that smell? Meeeeooowwww! The horrendous screech once more echoed through her whole being. Suddenly, the kind voices were there again. The 'pooming' stopped. The dreadful noise, albeit more demented, became more distant until it disappeared entirely.

The voices spoke calmly, soothingly. She meandered cautiously out of her bed, and all was still again. She felt safe. Time for breakfast – she loved those delicious yellow flakes. Scamper, scamper, over the luscious, deep, wood-chipped floor. Lap, lap as she sipped lovingly from the shiny, silver water fountain. Snuffle, snuffle, as she rummaged around to find the tastiest, largest pieces.

As she nibbled away, she contemplated today's plan. First: patrol the perimeter – another daily habit ingrained in her from her previous life – check vigilantly, looking for evidence of any breaks or damages that might present opportunities for escape. But as nothing ever seemed to change here now, her steady routine had tempered into little more than a gentle wander. She enjoyed the exercise – the opportunity to stretch her legs, explore the extents of her estate and take in the multitude of smells that wafted by. She loved to stand at the edge and wonder what was beyond – her 'happy place' where she felt like she was flying … over forests … over mountains … over seas … and over soft warm sands. And all from the comfort of her own home. Laughter. Joy. Bliss.

Her nose twitched – something familiar. As she stared searchingly out into the blur beyond the bars, she became aware of a dark shadow, skulkily rising and obscuring her view. Close. So close. Two penetratingly green orbs seemed to lurk deep in its midst. That smell.

Those orbs. That smell? Those orbs …. Totally hypnotised, her body stiffened. There was no tearing herself away. Never before had she been so paralysed with fear. Unable to run. No sense to hide. No reaction. No instinct.

Somewhere at the back of her mind, she thought … no she felt, she should know what to do. Observe? Hadn't she been looking for something? Looking … for a way to escape? Patrol? Wasn't that why she'd been searching? Searching … for a way to escape. What else … what else? A way to escape. But there was none. No escape. Paralysed. Paralysed. Paralysed. In all her preparation and training, had she ever known what was next? What followed? Observe. Patrol. But what next? Was this really how the rebellion should end? Was she truly face to face with the enemy? Revolution. Revenge. Justice! What did it even mean?

Meeeooowwwwwww! The shadow launched itself directly at General Fluffkins – the ground seemed to slide away from underneath her. For a brief moment, she was flying! A vicious frenzied, cloud of noise, teeth, hair and madness overwhelmed infinity. Poom! Poom! Poom! No respite, no relief. Everything was black.

Meeeooowwwwwww! Still, it continued. Poom! It went on. Yet, even so, amidst all the clamour and chaos, she was flying! Screech! ... Over forests. Meow! ... Over mountains. Poom! ... Over seas. Meow, meow, meow! ... Over soft warm sands. The world shook again and again ... but the shadow couldn't reach her. Those once oppressive bars ... were now her saviours. She was safe ... inside ... inside her enclosure and inside her thoughts.

Soon enough, the kind voices returned – more hurried and scrambled this time – but it wasn't long before silence descended peacefully once more. As General Fluffkins righted herself and brushed away misplaced bits of bedding and wood chip from her fur, she took a moment to reflect: What smells! What delights! Everything 'in here' was just entirely marvellous! Soon she would be gently lifted out for her daily exercise and snuggles, soon all would be well again. Ooo! A sunflower seed. Bliss.

We hope you have enjoyed Hamster Tales. Please vote for your favourite so that the winning author can be awarded their prize worth £50.

You can do this via our website, www.rulerswit.co.uk
by direct message through our Facebook page
or you can email, hello@rulerswit.co.uk

The Ruler's Wit team.

The Ruler's Wit Team

Donna Shepherd

Donna gained her BA and MA in English as a mature student at Loughborough University and runs her own business, Words by Red Kite. She also works as a development editor. Her website is: https://wordsbyredkite.com

Donna lives in North Warwickshire with her husband, daughter, Harry the rescue terrier and two rescue cats. A frequent character of Donna's stories is Tom the cat who in reality died six years ago and is still missed every day.

Melinda Ingram

Melinda gained an MA in English – Creative Writing at Loughborough University. She is a qualified teacher and has taught people aged two to sixty-two in a variety of settings. Melinda retired from the University of Leicester and now teaches part-time at a nearby FE College. She is also a trustee of her local community library. Melinda has edited and contributed chapters to books on education for Sage and Learning Matters (under Min Wilkie) including *Supporting Learning in Primary Schools* and *Doing Action Research*. She has self-published Fictionalising Iraq in British and American Literature (Children's and YA). Melinda's creative writing is often directed towards children and young people, reflecting her interest in life writing and time-slip stories.

Stevie Ashurst

Stevie has a BA Hons degree in Art and Design from Suffolk College and currently works as Senior Web Designer at Loughborough University. They have however been a keen writer and storyteller since being old enough to write. With an odd and sometimes surreal sense of humour, they enjoy writing stories of most genres and styles.

Stevie is a member of two writing groups – Bell's Shower and, of course, Ruler's Wit. Their website is: www.ash28.co.uk

Karen Ette

Karen completed her PhD at Loughborough University, where she also gained her MA in English, Creative Writing. She has since taught there on the MA Creative Writing course and on the third-year undergraduate publishing module.

Karen's novel, Don't Be Late in the Morning, was published in 2019. She has also written: A Second Christmas Truce?– Christmas on the Western Front, 1915, The Advent Calendar Recipe Book, and Your UCAS Application: a step-by-step guide.

Karen is a professional member of the Chartered Institute for Editors and Proofreaders and her website is:
www.the-writers-secret-helper.com

Printed in Great Britain
by Amazon

49010949R00086